EARNING THE MOUNTAIN MAN'S TRUST

BROTHERS OF SAPPHIRE RANCH
BOOK FOUR

MISTY M. BELLER

Misty M. Beller
BOOKS

Hope deferred makes the heart sick, But when the desire comes, it is a tree of life.

Proverbs 13:12 (NKJV)

CHAPTER 1

*E*ric LaGrange eyed the mountain slope still ahead of them. He rode with a group of Coulters, headed up this treacherous path toward their ranch. The blinding afternoon sun illuminated the snow-capped peaks to the west, its stark light only shadowed by the low-flying vulture circling overhead in search of its next meal.

This place reminded him too much of another steep slope. That jagged ledge was thousands of miles away from here, yet tragedy didn't care about location. Though he and his best friend had only been boys, daring to play in the spot they'd been warned against, his best friend's life had changed forever that day.

He couldn't let that happen to his daughter.

His *daughter*.

The word still sounded so foreign. How could he have had a child—been a father—for nearly a year and not known?

Shouldn't he have *felt* something? Somehow been different? Maybe sensed a gaping hole in his heart?

He *was* missing a part of his heart, but that piece had been gone for more than the ten months his daughter had been alive. A year and seven months, as a matter of fact. Since the last time he'd seen Naomi.

What he'd thought would only be a few weeks away to handle business while his father recovered from a surgical procedure had turned to four long months. Four months during which Naomi never responded to a single letter. And when he'd finally been allowed a short trip back to Wayneston to see her, she'd been gone.

He'd searched for months to no avail. There'd been no trace of her until two and a half months ago—telling him he had a daughter.

He'd come to Montana Territory to find what he'd lost.

The autumn air nipped at his exposed skin as he breathed in the chill. Colder weather would arrive sooner than he wished. How bitter the winters must be at these heights. His mount trudged upward, picking its way around the boulders scattered along the sharp mountainside.

As the trail widened, Dinah, Naomi's sister, slowed her horse to ride beside him, her expression concerned. "Eric, are you all right? You look pale."

He forced a smile. "Just lost in thought." He couldn't afford to show weakness, not when so much was at stake. He'd once thought Dinah a friend, back when he and Naomi were court-ing. The two were twins, but you wouldn't guess it to look at them. They possessed completely different personalities and tastes, yet they'd often known what the other was thinking.

Did Dinah's kindness to him now mean her sister would feel the same when he saw her again?

Maybe not.

He was not among friends, regardless how kind these Coulters had been to him. There were enough of them that Eric had been able to stay at the fringe during the two weeks they'd been traveling. Dinah and Jericho, along with Jericho's brothers, Jonah and Jude, plus Jude's intended, Angela, who seemed to be a newcomer here. There were two youngsters as well, the brothers' niece and nephew, Lillian and Sean. With so many, it was easy enough for Eric to keep to himself.

Dinah seemed fully entrenched in this place, having married Jericho Coulter. She had made a home on the Coulter ranch with the rest of these people. She was likely responsible for Naomi's engagement to Jericho's brother, Jonah.

Eric wouldn't be unkind to Dinah, but he also wouldn't confide in her.

As the trail narrowed around the side of a cliff, the group spread out single-file. He would have preferred to remain at the very back, but Jonah, Naomi's intended, slipped in behind him. One of the Coulter brothers always stayed near the lead, and another lingered near the tail of the group. Maybe they were being protective, but it felt like an effort to control the rest.

"Almost there." Jericho's voice sounded from the front.

Eric's body tightened. They'd built a house this close to a cliff? His daughter was being raised in conditions far more dangerous than he would have thought Naomi would allow.

Anger spurred through him. It wasn't as if she didn't have another choice. If she'd answered any one of his letters, he'd have dropped everything and come to her. They could have married immediately. He would have done whatever she needed.

Instead, she'd waited until six months passed to even tell him his daughter existed. Was it because of her impending marriage to Coulter that she finally sent word to him at all?

Maybe Eric should thank the man. Or not, for he'd also stolen the one woman Eric had ever loved.

"We're here!" The young girl's voice belonged to Lillian, the

Coulters' niece, who looked to be about twelve. "There's Naomi." The riders in front fanned out as they entered a clearing.

Eric's insides squeezed tighter. He would see her in less than a minute.

Would she look the same? What would she think about his appearance? What would she say to him? Her letter had been to the point, stating facts like she was reporting a news story.

Where was the gentle, faithful woman he'd known? Where was the heart? The love? Gone, apparently. Or maybe given to the Coulter brother who'd been sending Eric narrow-eyed looks for two long weeks. As if *Eric* was the one in the wrong.

They entered the yard, and several buildings came into view, but a commotion at the corral drew his attention.

A young woman with a familiar willowy figure struggled to close a gate. The horse on the other side pushed, determined to charge out of the corral.

And no wonder.

Eric's breath came harder. Another horse occupied the corral, kicking out furiously with its hind legs. Forcing the other horse against the gate that Naomi was trying to close.

Eric had to get to her. Now.

"Let them out!" Jericho pushed his horse forward at the same time Eric dug in his heels, pushing his tired gelding into a lope.

Faster. But after two weeks on the trail, his mount was incapable. If only he had Gypsy. Naomi needed help.

This time, Eric had to be there for her.

At last, he reached the corral.

Two of the Coulter brothers had already leapt from their horses.

The gate swung loose, and a horse ran free on the other side of the yard. Where was Naomi?

The form on the ground caught his gaze.

Jericho was already dropping to his knees.

Eric leaped from his horse and sprinted toward them. Had the horse trampled her? She lay so still.

God, help her.

The others reached her moments after Eric did, and Dinah pushed through to kneel at her sister's side. Dinah had been a doctor back in Wayneston, so maybe she'd know how to help better than he. He shifted closer to Naomi's feet so he wouldn't be in the way.

Naomi pushed up to her elbows. "I'm all right." Her face was pale, her voice sounded far from steady, but she was alert.

Thank you, God.

Eric's heart hammered as he took her in. So familiar, yet different. She was thinner than he remembered, and she'd added a few fine lines at her eyes.

But those eyes. They were still just as wide and deep brown. Like the James River on the summer night he'd asked her to marry him. He could still remember how her smile had lit them from within and held him so transfixed that he'd had no desire to look away.

Dinah spouted medical questions that had Naomi rolling those eyes in a way that was so familiar it ached.

He itched to reach out. To touch her face. To hold her the way he once had.

Eric started to edge around to her other side, but Jonah beat him to the spot, crouching beside her. He placed his hand on her shoulder, and it took everything in Eric not to step forward and jerk the man away.

Naomi hadn't even seen him yet. She was too focused on her sister and Jonah.

Her *intended.*

Clenching his fists, Eric forced himself to look up, over the crowed, and breathe. He scanned the ranch yard. The log buildings sat on a hill, with the house at the upper part of the clearing, the barn and corrals down the slope. The homestead was not nearly as large as he'd expected for a family this size.

The door of the house opened, and he waited to see who would emerge. From what he understood, aside from Naomi and the baby, three other Coulter brothers had remained at the ranch while Jericho, Jude, and Jonah traveled. Also an elderly Indian man and woman had come to help Naomi and act as chaperones. They were the parents of Two Stones, a fellow Eric had briefly met when he arrived in Fort Benton. Two Stones and his wife had planned to stay in town a few more days to finish business, but they'd return eventually. Neither the three Coulter brothers nor the elderly couple had appeared yet to check on this commotion. Were they all away from the house? What about his daughter?

He shifted his focus back at Naomi. But in the next moment, movement caught his eye again by the door. Maybe the native woman, if she'd stayed behind with Naomi.

But it wasn't a white-haired grandmother. The tiny figure who appeared couldn't be more than a year old, and even from this distance he could make out the fringe of reddish curls.

His breath stalled, and his body froze in place as he took in every part of her.

Not that he could make out many details. She wore a dress that fell to her knees with pants underneath. She had pudgy cheeks and pale skin, and he longed to get closer, to get a better look. To pull her into his arms and hug her to his chest.

The entire vision was...beautiful. Warmth spread through his chest, unexpected and mysterious, as if his body comprehended something his mind was only beginning to grasp. He was filled with a love so powerful that his heart might explode.

Who knew a man could feel such intense emotions?

The tiny girl turned around knelt in the doorway, then slid a leg down to the stoop. Her next foot reached down to the ground.

Was she leaving the house? Who was supposed to be watching her?

No adult appeared in the cabin door.

Eric's pulse surged. She could get hurt.

He sprinted up the hill.

She found her balance on the slope and was toddling down toward him. Running, that was. Down this steep grade. Any moment she could trip and tumble forward, rolling downward.

Memory flashed of the last time he'd watched someone topple down a mountain.

Nathan had never walked again.

And she was just a baby.

At last he reached her, gripping her shoulders to stop her forward motion. "Whoa there. Not so fast." He dropped to his knees in front of her.

She regarded him with wary eyes. Wide, brown eyes, just like Naomi's.

A knot clogged his throat.

His baby girl.

She started to back away from him, pulling from his hold. Was she afraid of him?

He had to say something. Quick. He couldn't let her be frightened.

He managed to force out a word. "Hello." His voice came out rough and scratchy, so he cleared it.

She stopped backing up but still eyed him with suspicion.

He smiled. "Are you Mary Ellen?"

The distrust in those big brown eyes melted into curiosity. "Me-me." She patted her chest with chubby fingers.

Her voice was the sweetest symphony he could hope to hear. Emotions tumbled inside him, joy and fear and elation and regret. This tiny being before him, with curls like autumn leaves and eyes like clear pools, was his child. His flesh and blood.

He extended a hand to her, palm up, an offer as much as an

invitation. "I'm your papa. I've come a very long way to meet you."

Mary Ellen gazed at his hand, then back up to his face. She didn't speak again, but no hint of wariness remained in her gaze. At least she wasn't afraid of him. That seemed a good first step.

She shifted her attention past him, and her eyes lit. "Ma-ma."

He turned to look down the slope toward the group still gathered in front of the corral. No one even realized the child had come outside on her own.

Whatever Naomi had been doing with the horses had clearly taken her away from caring for their daughter. Such errors in judgment could be disastrous for a child.

Now that he'd finally been united with his daughter, he would make sure she was protected. This wild land was much too dangerous, especially for a child so young.

His life had just shifted. Everything that had seemed important to him before meant nothing anymore. From now on, nothing mattered more than making sure his little one was safe.

CHAPTER 2

O f all the times to find oneself face down in the dirt. Naomi's body protested as she worked to push herself up to sitting, the effects of being nearly run over by that new mare still reverberating through her bones.

"Before you get up, there's something I need to tell you." Dinah's voice took on her big-sister tone. Probably she wanted to make her allow help back to the house. Sometimes Dinah could be a bit over-bearing when she donned her doctor's smock—even figuratively.

Naomi ignored her and stood, pausing to let her swimming vision settle as she glanced around at those around her. She'd not expected the group to return from Fort Benton so soon. A few more days at least.

And...hadn't there been a face among she'd not expected? Her heart picked up speed again. It couldn't be who she'd imagined in that quick glance. But where was he?

She scanned the area in front of the barn and corral, then up the slope to the house.

There.

A man stood near the cabin, his frame silhouetted against the afternoon light. Mary Ellen stood next to him.

Eric. Her heart knew it, even before she shifted her focus back to him. Those shoulders, wide but not brawny. The way he stood as if ready for action. Prepared to step in and make the world a better place.

He'd come. After all this time. She had dreamed of this moment for so long, but now that it was reality, the situation felt like a cruel twist of fate.

She'd already agreed to marry Jonah.

As she watched him now, his focus was entirely on their daughter, Mary Ellen.

Their daughter. He'd finally come, and she hadn't even been able to introduce him to their daughter. Their flesh and blood. Every time she looked at Mary Ellen's red curls, she saw Eric's auburn waves.

And now to watch them side by side... So many could-have-beens played through her mind. The home she'd once imagined they'd have together. The life they'd create. She'd once imagined him cradling their babies. Looking up at her with those tender, loving eyes.

Yet that had never happened. Instead, he'd turned his back on her.

She limped slowly up the hill, each step a painful reminder of how frail she'd let herself become. Jonah, good man that he was, steadied her with his hand on her arm. Her bruised body protested, but it was the ache in her heart that truly weighed her down.

As she approached, Mary Ellen turned to her. "Ma-ma." The child started toward her with those unsteady steps.

Before she could lift a hand and tell her daughter to wait, Eric grabbed Mary Ellen's arm, pulling her back.

"It's too dangerous." His voice was stern, though not loud. The way his eyes sparked as he glared at Naomi, though, it seemed he intended the rebuke for her.

Resentment flared. She'd planned to stop Mary Ellen herself, not let her take a tumble.

She marched the last few steps up the hill, her defenses fortified. She'd wanted Eric to come, but he still had a lot to explain. And even more to make up for.

She stopped in front of him, downhill unfortunately, so he towered over her.

Jonah stood at her side, his hand moving from her arm to her back, his touch reassuring.

Jonah was always considerate like that.

Unlike Eric, who'd deserted her without a word, only a day after they'd done something she never thought she'd allow.

And now, he stood before her.

Looking different, yet exactly the same. Older, more...seasoned. But that rich auburn hair, the perfect angle of his cheekbones. Those eyes. They'd always looked at her with such warmth, like she would be safe with him.

The warmth was shielded behind sparks now. And barely concealed suspicion.

She raised her chin, meeting his gaze. She was the one who'd suffered to bring their daughter into the world. From casting up every meal for two months, to unbelievable pain and worry as she gave birth—in the woods of all places, on the side of a mountain road.

Then long exhausting nights. Realizing Mary Ellen really was Eric's, not...

She sucked in a breath. She couldn't let herself think about that other possibility right now. She couldn't let that dirtiness creep in. Not if she was going to manage this meeting with any amount of courage.

Eric studied her. Maybe waiting for her to speak first.

"Eric." She was pleased that her voice sounded strong.

His expression turned unreadable. "Naomi." His voice sounded guarded.

She took a deep breath, pushing down her anger. She could be decent and civil. "You've finally come." Perhaps that was stretching *civil*.

Definitely sparks in his eyes. "To find my daughter wandering from the house by herself. She tried to run down this mountainside and nearly fell. If she had, her head could have hit a rock. She could have died."

Anger surged, but she grabbed her control just in time. She and Eric had created this beautiful child together, yet *she* had borne the burden of raising her alone. And now, here he stood, acting like some great protector, as if he'd always been here. As if he'd never left her side.

She was still searching for a fair response when Jonah's voice ground out beside her. "You'd best keep it respectful. And I'd think twice about accusing someone of not doing what you haven't been around to do yourself." The warning in both his words and tone were impossible to ignore.

Eric regarded Jonah, and she could hardly breathe as she watched him. Would he rile even more at that barely-veiled attack?

These two had just traveled from Fort Benton together, which was probably what Dinah had been trying to tell her when Naomi had hurried to stand up earlier. That would be a journey of at least two weeks. Had they been civil to each other all that time? Or had resentment festered between them on the trail? She could feel anger seething from Jonah, though he kept it in check. She didn't dare take her eyes off Eric as he eyed Jonah with a calculating expression.

Whatever passed between the two of them seemed to be what Eric needed in order for his tension to ease a little. His gaze moved back to her, and he gave a tight nod. "He's right. I haven't been here, though that certainly wasn't my choice. I would have come if I'd known." His voice tensed again, but then he breathed out. "You did bear all the weight of raising her. Now that I'm here, I intend to do my part."

She'd done more than raise the child. Getting the babe to the point of being born alive had been almost harder than the months afterward. But a man wouldn't think of that.

And what did he mean, he intended to do his part? Did he plan to stay? Because there was no way under the sun, moon, and stars she would allow him to take her daughter away from her.

And she wasn't leaving these mountains. The peace of this place had changed her.

Her hands trembled, the need to hold her daughter taking over in a rush so quick that she could think of nothing else. She smiled down at Mary Ellen, who stood looking at them uncertainly, her hand still in Eric's grip.

Mary Ellen's little cheeks appled in a relieved smile. She started forward, slipping from Eric's grasp. He must not have been expecting her to pull away. Either that or he was allowing her to go to Naomi.

She bent low and scooped up Mary Ellen, holding her close, breathing in the scent of sleep that always lingered after she awoke from a nap. The feel of her, the solidness, centered Naomi. This wasn't such an awful thing. She'd wanted Eric to come. He needed to know his daughter, and this sweet bundle needed her father.

After inhaling another steadying breath, she turned back to Eric. "Running Woman was napping in the room with Mary Ellen. She must still be asleep. Mary Ellen has just learned how to open door latches."

Eric's brows lowered. "We need to find a different way to secure the doors then."

As if she wasn't doing enough to keep her daughter safe. Couldn't he see how perfectly healthy and happy Mary Ellen was? Couldn't he see how much Naomi had already done—by herself, thank you very much?

She tried to keep her voice even. "She's just learned the trick this week. I've been placing a chair in front of the door to the bed chamber when she sleeps, but I didn't want to do that with Running Woman in the room. She's elderly and might not be strong enough to push it aside." The woman had never fully recovered her strength after a hard fight against smallpox last year.

Eric shook his head with a tight smile. "I'll see to something more secure."

"*I'll* see to something more secure." Jonah's voice held warning. "It's our house, after all."

The way he said *our* made it sound like he meant the two of them. As if she and Jonah lived there as man and wife, even though they weren't married yet.

Heat flared up her neck, and she fumbled for a way to make the point clear. "The Coulter home, that is. Jericho and Dinah have one of the rooms, and I sleep in the other with Mary Ellen." But while her sister and brother-in-law had been gone, Two Stones's parents had been kind enough to stay here with her. Chaperones of sorts, since the only other people on the ranch were Jonah's three younger brothers.

Jonah straightened, his hand dropping from her back. She glanced at him in time to see a flash of hurt beneath his anger. Had she injured him with her explanation?

"The point is"—Jonah's voice was hard—"this is not *your* home to come in and make changes. Naomi is not *your* woman. Mary Ellen might be your flesh and blood, but you've not done anything to help with her, not in the hard months when Naomi carried her, not during her birth, and not for any moment since then. You might have a small claim on her—a *tiny* claim—but if you intend to have any part in her life, you'd best come here with your hat in your hands respectfully."

Tension crackled between them. The rest of the group had gathered around and beside her, but no one spoke.

Eric glared at Jonah, and when Jonah glared back, there was no calming effect.

The fire in Eric's eyes could have lit a campfire. "You think I wanted to be left in the dark? You think I wanted to miss the first *year* of my daughter's life? I would have dropped everything—changed *everything*—to be with her. I would have found the best doctors for her, taken all the hardest parts on myself." His voice nearly shook with intensity. He stepped closer to Jonah, and though his voice was lower, the words hummed with intensity. "Now that I'm here, I can promise you this. No man— not you and all your brothers combined—is going to keep me from taking care of my daughter the way I see fit."

Emotions whirled through Naomi.

Changed his entire life *for her*. Found the best doctors... *for her*.

It almost seemed like he meant Naomi, not just their daughter.

Jonah stepped forward.

By the time she realized why...he was swinging.

His fist slammed into Eric's jaw.

CHAPTER 3

*E*ric's vision blurred.

Pain and anger surged together, unleashing a flood of pent-up fury.

Returning the punch came as instinct borne of a thousand fights with his cousin Harvey.

Eric swung hard with his right, then jabbed with his left. Keep him off-balance. Keep it coming. Muscle memory, etched deep in his core. Only a pounding would stop his cousin. Eric would pummel until he pinned Harvey to the ground.

But this wasn't Harvey.

Jonah was no youth. From the thick cord of his neck to the solid steel in his middle, this man knew how to fight back. Each blow plunged Eric's head back, sending flashes of light through his vision or knocking the breath from his lungs.

Voices around them called for the fighting to stop, but they were so distant, his instincts pushed through every call to cease.

Fury, pent up and growing, feeding in the months since he'd received Naomi's letter, fueled him. He had a daughter Naomi had never told him about, and now these people were trying to keep her from him. They had exposed his child to all the dangers in this wilderness and wouldn't even let Eric step in to protect her.

He landed a blow in Coulter's face, feeling a satisfying crack. Lecherous snake thought he could force his way into Naomi life, into the babe's life. Take over Eric's rights and responsibilities. Let this be a lesson to him.

Coulter rammed a fist into Eric's gut. The force shot pain through his core, up his spine, into his chest. He doubled over and clutched his middle.

He had to straighten. Had to prepare himself, and not just for another blow. He had to attack.

"Enough!"

Jericho's voice boomed, slicing through the pain and his body's panic as he struggled for breath. The words sounded like they came from a distance, but they cut through the fog in his mind.

"This solves nothing," the oldest brother said. "And fighting will not be tolerated on our ranch."

At last, a bit of air seeped in, but Eric's body demanded more. He sucked another breath, then another, each inhalation a ragged draw that seared his ribs like a torch. The world slowly solidified around him, the edges of objects sharpening as his head cleared.

He finally managed to straighten. At least he was still on his feet, though he wasn't sure for how long.

Coulter panted too, blood trickling from his nose and running into his beard.

The fury that had fueled Eric ebbed away, leaving a hollow ache in its place. Especially when he glanced at Naomi, standing near Coulter—her intended—holding their daughter.

Mary Ellen wailed, and Naomi bounced her, trying to soothe her. They shouldn't have fought in front of the child.

Naomi's sister stood at Coulter's other side, lifting a cloth to his nose. He started to wave her away, but Dinah pressed harder, and Coulter allowed her help.

Dinah, who used to be his friend.

Naomi, who'd once promised to marry him.

Both had chosen Coulters.

Eric had never felt so much an outsider, especially with Jericho glaring his way. It helped a little that the man shot the same hard look to his younger brother, the cad with a woman on each side, coddling him.

Jericho finally focused on Eric, his voice stern but no longer shouting. "You'd best leave now. I understand you want to see your daughter, but you need a level head to do so. Come back tomorrow noon." His hard edge softened a little. "We'll work this out, but make sure you bring your patience."

Eric's heart still pounded, but he could breathe better. As much as he'd like to finish this with Coulter here and now, Jericho was right. He didn't need a fight. He'd come all this way to get to know his daughter. Brawling would only drive a wedge between himself and Naomi. He'd not come with the intention of trying to win her back, not after she'd spurned all his attempts to contact her and was now to be married to another man, but they needed to be amicable. They shared a daughter, after all.

He nodded, but the pain that shot up from the base of his neck made him immediately regret the motion. "Tomorrow then." His voice didn't come out as strong as he would have liked, but he didn't try to say more.

He slid one last look at Naomi before turning away. She was staring at him with a stricken look in those wide brown eyes. A new stab of pain twisted inside him. He'd not meant to hurt her. Even if she wanted nothing to do with him, he didn't wish to hurt her.

He turned away and started down the hill. His gelding grazed at the edge of the trees, so he aimed toward it. The animal let him grab the reins without having to chase him, thank goodness. He wouldn't attempt to mount where the others could see him. The way his body already ached, his climbing on the horse might not be a pleasant sight. His middle burned, and he feared Coulter had cracked a rib or two.

When he'd led the horse far enough for the woods to shield him, he positioned the animal downhill from him and raised his left foot to the stirrup. The burning in his chest heated, and when he pulled himself into the saddle, the pain lit to an open flame, searing his insides.

He bent forward, forcing air into his lungs, though it felt like he was inhaling flame.

The horse started forward, and Eric managed to make sure they aimed away from the house. Where should he go?

Pain fogged his mind. Hadn't Jude said the nearest town was a full day's ride? He couldn't go that far. He'd expected there would at least be other houses near the ranch.

Yet he'd not seen a single person during their ride that day. Maybe if his horse kept walking, they'd stumble onto a homestead.

As the gelding maneuvered down the slope at an angle, Eric had to take a more active role in the ride, guiding the animal around low-hanging tree limbs and keeping him to a walk when the horse tried to trot down the steeper sections.

Time stretched at a painful pace as they rode to the base of the hill and along the creek that ran between two slopes. Should he follow the creek or start up the other incline? They'd ridden beside a stream like this one during the first part of their travel that morning, but as far as he could remember, they'd not crossed to the opposite side at all. Maybe he should head that way in search of neighbors. Someone might let him sleep in their barn.

Would he be able to find his way back to the ranch tomorrow if he went too far?

No matter what, he had to be there at noon to see his daughter. Perhaps he'd ignore Naomi and the Coulter men completely so he didn't accidentally get himself in trouble. He didn't need to talk to them, at least not yet. He could keep his focus and his words aimed at Mary Ellen.

As the sun slid beyond the peak of the hill they climbed, he reached a spot where the trees opened to a small clearing and the ground leveled off a little. Maybe he should just sleep here tonight. He had his bedding and a bit of food in the packs tied onto his saddle, enough to make it through one night anyway.

He allowed the gelding to stop in the grassy area, and the animal immediately lowered its head to graze. Eric tensed for the fresh surge of pain that would come when he dismounted. As he clenched his middle to lift his leg over the horse's back, the fire inside stole his breath and most of the strength from his bones.

He made it to the ground, then sank to his knees and toppled onto his side. He gripped his arms around his middle. Every breath hurt, yet his lungs craved the air. His jaw ached. His belly churned.

Maybe he should stay like this all night, curled on his side. The horse could graze as long as it wanted, though it would be kinder to the animal if he could at least remove the bit and loosen the girth.

And Eric should get his blankets. The late afternoon air was already chilled. Who knew how cold it would get that night?

For now, he would lie here. He could get the blanket in a minute. At least the pain in his body could distract his mind from the stronger ache of knowing how messed up his life had become.

He had a daughter. A *daughter*. And she didn't even know him.

He'd worked so hard in his father's business. He always took the right path. He *always* did the right thing, no matter how hard it was. That one night when he'd let himself go too far with Naomi had been his only moral breach.

Well, the only one since he was a kid.

And look where it had brought him. Even with all the other good Eric had worked so hard to do, look what had become of him.

He was lying on the side of a mountain, curled up in pain. His daughter lived in another man's home, and the woman he still loved—had always loved and would always love—planned to marry that man.

The love of his life and the daughter they'd created were both in the arms of another man while he lay out here in the cold.

No one in this wilderness cared enough to come check on him.

How had his life come to this?

And the bigger question...

What was he going to do about it?

CHAPTER 4

*N*aomi fumbled the last slice of potato, which bounced off the side of the stewpot before plopping inside. With her insides in such turmoil and her hands trembling, it was a wonder she hadn't cut herself chopping the vegetables. Her thoughts, like her midsection, refused to settle. The heat from the cookstove didn't help any, making her shirtwaist cling to her sweat-dampened underarms and back.

She glanced at Mary Ellen, who sat on the rug, stacking another block onto her growing tower.

Running Woman was watching from the rocking chair, a smile curving the lines at her eyes. She and her husband would stay until Two Stones and Heidi returned from Fort Benton, then ride on to their village with them.

The older woman had been such a help while Dinah and the others were away. A diligent guardian, even with Mary Ellen's constant activity.

Eric had simply arrived at the worst of moments earlier. That new mare had jumped the corral fence again, and since Mary Ellen and Running Woman had both been sleeping soundly, Naomi had gone out to catch the horse and put her back in the pen. She'd never expected sweet Pepper, the gangly mule Jericho had purchased to stay with the cattle and protect them, to start up a kicking fit. Clearly, the donkey felt the need to protect herself from the new mare.

Of course, the horse had been determined to escape the beating.

Naomi should have released the gate sooner, but her instincts had pushed her to keep the animal in.

She'd not had the chance to explain any of that to Eric, though perhaps it wouldn't have altered his thinking about her mothering abilities. He probably would have said she should have left the horse alone until one of the men returned to catch it.

And maybe she should have.

She let out a sigh as she stirred the soup. Being a parent was a constant barrage of decisions, and no matter what she chose, she always second-guessed herself. Should she ignore Mary Ellen's occasional temper tantrums so as not to reward the action with her attention? Or should she reprimand the child, making sure she knew such behavior wasn't good?

"What can I do to help?" Dinah stepped up beside her.

Naomi hadn't even heard her sister come in the front door. She should have been more aware. Maybe Eric was right about her not being a good protector.

Naomi motioned toward the cloth covering the warm bread on the work counter. "Could you slice that loaf?"

Dinah reached for a knife, then lifted the fabric to release the savory scent of sourdough. Simply having another person in the kitchen, helping bear the load, eased some of the tension in Naomi's shoulders. As she stirred the stew, she let her gaze linger on Dinah's work, the knife slicing through the bread with a practiced hand, each piece falling neatly beside the one before it.

The tower of blocks succumbed to the height, tumbling, and

Mary Ellen giggled. The familiar sights and sounds and smells should make her feel better, but they reminded her of what was at stake.

Jonah had been hurt—Dinah mentioned a broken nose—but he insisted it was nothing more than the weariness of their journey that sent him to bed early. It was clear he wanted to be alone, so she'd not followed him out to the bunkhouse to make sure he was comfortable.

He'd been injured trying to protect her. Should she have insisted on doing more to help him?

She hadn't actually *needed* protecting. Not from Eric. She could stand up for herself. He wouldn't hurt her, and though his superior attitude had grated, his words hadn't actually harmed her.

Where was Eric now? Wandering the mountains? What if he'd been hurt badly? What if he was lying in the woods somewhere, curled in pain and unable to care for himself?

Jonah had all his brothers and Dinah and Naomi, not to mention a roof over his head, and a fire in the hearth, and someone to deliver him food and drink.

Who did Eric have? What if he wasn't all right?

"What are you thinking, Na?" Dinah's voice pressed into her thoughts.

Tears pricked her eyes at the thought of putting to words these awful possibilities. Perhaps Dinah could help, though. She inhaled a breath. "What if Eric is hurt? What if he needs help?"

Dinah was quiet a minute as she sliced the last of the loaf. when she spoke, her words came softly. "I've been wondering the same thing." She didn't look at Naomi, but her tone was thoughtful as she arranged the pieces on a platter. "He took some hard blows to his head and abdomen. That last one especially—it may have cracked ribs."

Naomi's own middle tightened. "But he walked away. That's a good sign, isn't it?" Though Jonah had started the fisticuffs,

Eric had done nothing to stop the violence. Even if Dinah didn't approve of the fight, at least her doctor's concern kept her from being prejudiced against him. She could trust her sister to want the best for him—physically, at least.

"True." Dinah word emerged slowly. "A broken rib would be painful, but it would heal without the need for help. As long as the rib doesn't puncture internal organs."

Panic gripped Naomi's chest. "How do we know if that's happened?"

Dinah put a hand on her arm. "It's unlikely."

"But if it happens, he'll need help, right? We have to check on him."

Dinah held her gaze, and too much fear churned inside Naomi to hide it from her sister. Dinah's eyes glistened, and she nodded. "I'll see if Jericho can follow his tracks. I can tell him what to look for when he finds Eric. If anything serious is wrong, he can bring him back here."

"Will you go with him? Please? If Eric has organ damage, you'll need to treat him there, won't you?"

Dinah's mouth pinched, but the corners tugged a little. "I'll go with him." She moved to the washbasin to scrub her hands.

Naomi eased out a long breath. Now that Dinah had a mission, she would carry it out quickly. She would make sure Eric wasn't suffering. That his injuries weren't severe.

And that was all Naomi wanted, right? After all, she'd agreed to marry Jonah. She could be civil to Eric, even friendly, but she couldn't love him. She had to work harder at squelching that emotion.

Yet it seemed impossible.

She wanted Eric *here*. To meet his daughter. To help her stack blocks on the floor and give her a horsie ride on his legs. To look up at Naomi with that tenderness that made her insides melt. The expression that said she meant everything to him. That he treasured her and would never leave.

The stinging pricked her eyes again. She could never have the happy scene she was imagining, not without it being tainted with all the tears and heartache that came after he'd abandoned her.

She had to come to terms with this reality they faced. And decide what was truly best for herself and her daughter.

* * *

*E*ric's consciousness stirred as a firm hand gripped on his shoulder. Voices sounded in the distance. A woman's. And a man's.

The grip rocked his shoulder, shooting pain through his body. The strength of it drew him from the remaining clutches of sleep. He opened his eyes to a world blurred at the edges. Then the form in the middle came sharper.

A man. Black haired with the look of a native.

Eric tried to sit upright, but the effort sent a fiery pain through his ribs. He clutched the place, squeezing his eyes closed as he waited out the blaze inside.

"Easy, friend." The voice was familiar.

He cracked his eyelids. The Coulters' friend he'd met in the town. "Two Stones." He mumbled the name, relaxing against the dirt and letting his eyes shut again.

"Yes. And Heidi. It is good we came this path and found you. Else your spilled blood might have drawn an animal who would not be as gentle as I am."

Eric parted his eyelids again. "Blood?" He'd thought all his wounds were inside.

Two Stones touched the corner of Eric's mouth with a finger, leaving behind a slight ache that came nowhere near that in his belly. "Your lip is split." He ran that same finger over Eric's hand. "And flesh missing here."

Eric shifted his hand to view the spot. Three knuckles with

the skin peeling. The reminder of the fight soaked over him like sour milk, bringing back all the frustrations. He would do better tomorrow.

He squinted at the sun shining through the treetops. "Is it still daylight?" He needed to relieve his horse of the saddle and bridle.

Two Stones followed his look to the sun. "The sun is two fingers from the noon mark."

Eric eyed him. Two fingers from...noon? Had he slept...? "Is it morning? Did I sleep all night?"

The chill in his bones knew the answer even before Two Stones spoke. "Yes."

Eric rolled onto his side, grabbing grass and pulling in order to move without using his belly muscles. "I have to get..." He fought back a groan as he pushed himself up on his hands and knees. "...to Mary Ellen."

He couldn't lose the chance to see his daughter.

"Why don't you eat first?" The woman crouched before him. "Here's some cammas bread. It will give you strength." She hadn't talked much back in Fort Benton, but so many other people had been around.

She held out a chunk of bread with an expression of compassion that made her feel more like a friend than anyone else he'd met since stepping off the steamboat.

He shifted into a sitting position, then eased out a long, slow breath before taking the food from her.

Two Stones crouched before him. The same friendliness his wife had just offered formed in his expression. "Will you tell me what happened?"

Eric swallowed his first bite, then managed to explain about the meeting and the fight in a few sentences. "Jericho said I could come back at noon today." He glanced back at the position of the sun, but he didn't have his bearings enough to use it to decipher what the time might be.

27

"We can be there." Two Stones motioned toward Eric's face. "And there is even time for you to wash." His eyes crinkled at the edges in the hint of a smile.

Eric accepted a larger piece of bread from Mrs. Two Stones —did they have a surname? He couldn't remember how she'd been introduced. His brain must still be addled from yesterday's pounding.

After giving him the rest of the food, which tasted more like fruit cake than bread, she moved away for a moment, then returned with a wet cloth. "You can wipe your face with this. Careful you don't scrape the scab from your lip. It may start bleeding again."

He accepted the rag and wiped the blessed coolness over his face. As good as it felt, the cold started his limbs trembling.

Two Stones must have noticed. "God did not let the ground freeze. That was a gift to you."

Eric eyed the man as he eased the cloth across the dried blood on his chin. "I suppose." The way he felt now didn't seem like a blessing from heaven, but things would be worse if he'd frozen in the night like a block of ice.

He finished wiping the crusted mess from his hands, too, then glanced between the pair. "Do I look more presentable?"

Two Stones didn't smile, but his wife did. Then she glanced up at her husband as though not sure which of them should answer.

Two Stones took the lead with a single nod. "Will do."

Not great then.

He moved onto his hands and knees again, then worked his way up to standing, clutching his ribs as he straightened.

The couple's horses stood grazing a few steps away, along with his own gelding, whose reins were tied to one of their saddles.

He started toward them. "Thanks for catching my horse."

Two Stones walked at his side. "We saw him drinking at the

creek. The dirt on his saddle told us he had been wandering all night. That is why we search for you."

He glanced over, and Two Stones met his gaze with one that seemed both understanding and frank. "Thank you for that. I might not have wakened if you hadn't come." And missing time with his daughter would be the real tragedy in that.

Two Stones held Eric's horse while he mounted, and it took everything he had not to groan with the effort. When he made it into the saddle, he kept one hand around his middle to hold his insides together while he gathered his reins with the other.

"We need to make sure Doc Dinah checks your injuries when we get to the ranch." Mrs. Two Stones waited beside her horse until her husband came to assist.

"You're going to the ranch?" He eyed them. "Is it on your way home?" Hadn't Jude said they lived in a native village a few hours away from the Coulters' place?

Two Stones nodded. "We will see you reach it in safety. Then we will ride with my father and mother to our village."

He wanted to protest, but the way he felt, when the terrain grew steep, he might topple off the horse. And he wasn't altogether sure he could find the clearing where the house and barn sat.

A thankful nod was all he could manage without letting another groan escape his lips. The bread had grounded him some, but the aches in his body still screamed.

Somehow, he had to regain his strength of will before they reached the ranch.

CHAPTER 5

*E*ric gritted his teeth against the pain as they set off down the slope, weaving through the trees. Two Stones led the way, and his wife rode behind Eric. It seemed all these people felt the need to surround him on the trail. Did he look so much the weakling? In truth, he felt fragile as a newborn right now—thankful for the protective way they sandwiched him.

When they reached the base of the mountain where he'd slept, Two Stones stopped to let the horses drink in the creek. As Eric's gelding gulped greedily, the other man studied him. "Do you have a better place to sleep this night than the cold ground?"

"I had hoped to stay at the Coulters' ranch. Maybe in their barn or something." Jude had intimated they had places he could sleep, though he'd never made an official offer. He pressed a hand to his ribs. "I'm guessing that's not an option anymore." He focused forward and set his jaw. "I can pitch a tent and build a campfire." He wasn't usually as weak as last night's collapse made him look. Sure, his nights away from home were usually spent in hotels—with soft beds and restaurant meals—but he'd made this journey all the way from Washington D.C. He might be accustomed to luxury, but he could handle sleeping on the ground until he worked out a better situation.

The captain of the steamer he'd traveled on to Fort Benton said his was one of the last boats going west before the Missouri River froze for the winter. Eric had wired his father from the tiny town when he'd disembarked, letting him know he would be gone longer than the six months he'd anticipated. Aside from two months each direction on the Missouri, he'd thought he could work things out with Naomi in a couple months. But he'd have to wait for the river to thaw now, which meant an extra three or four months at least. He'd promised to continue the negotiations he was working on through telegram though.

Which would be a challenge since the nearest town was a full day's ride away. At least, according to Jude, Missoula Mills possessed a telegraph.

They'd started up the opposite slope before Two Stones spoke again. The path proved wide enough for two to ride abreast, and Two Stones kept his spotted horse beside Eric's gelding.

"The days grow short and cold. The weather can turn quickly, and the mountains show no mercy. It is not good to sleep without shelter."

Eric shot the man a look. "Is there a house around here I can use?" The words came out a bit more jaded than they should have.

But this place was so much more remote than he'd imagined. And he'd burned the bridge of staying with the Coulters, at least for now. Not that he'd started the fight—Jonah had struck the first blow. But Eric had returned every punch.

He'd have to work to rebuild friendly relations with them. Though whether he'd ever feel like he could stay there without imposing—and without having to watch his back—remained to be seen.

"Our village is two hours from the ranch." Two Stones's voice turned earnest. "You are welcome to stay with us. We have warm lodges, good food, and pleasant company."

Eric's first instinct was to decline. His pride, the same stubborn pride that had him holding his middle together as if sheer will could mend bone and sinew. Yet as much as he'd like to assert his independence, another cold night without decent shelter would be torture.

Yet *two hours away*. How could he get to know his daughter with such a long trail between them?

"Your offer is generous. I thank you, but I fear the distance might be too far."

Two Stones nodded. "You are welcome any time."

When they reached the cliff where the horses had to travel single file, Eric's insides knotted, and not just because of the danger of falling. They were almost to the Coulter ranch. He would see his daughter, but he'd also be faced with the results of his hot-headed actions yesterday.

Would Jonah meet him at rifle-point and tell him to leave? The man had the right, since it was his ranch. Maybe his elder brother's steady head would win out. Hopefully, they'd keep to the promise Jericho had made yesterday.

Eric glanced upward. It was hard to tell in the midst of these trees, but the sun looked close to the noon mark. He would arrive pretty much when Jericho said for him to. They'd let him see his daughter, wouldn't they?

He'd have to face Naomi too. Not just her anger and hurt, but also her beauty and the many reminders of what they'd once had. The promises they'd once made to each other.

All of which she'd broken.

He couldn't let those thoughts in today. He had to keep a level head. If he focused on Mary Ellen alone, he wouldn't risk his temper rising. Or saying things that might anger the adults.

His only goal here was to get to know his daughter. He had to focus on that alone.

When they finally rode into the clearing, Jericho stood by the corral fence, not far from where Naomi had struggled with the horse the day before. Images of her on the ground surged in, but Eric pushed them back, keeping his attention on the man.

Two Stones rode on his left, the man's wife on his right. Their support was a gift he fully understood only as Jericho's hard expression softened.

They all reined in before him, and Two Stones dismounted immediately. "Jericho." He stepped forward and clasped hands with Coulter, then turned and motioned to Eric. "We found him sleeping in the cold and were glad to journey this last hour together."

As Two Stones moved to his wife's horse to help her dismount, Jericho focused on Eric.

Eric nodded a greeting, but his mind wouldn't summon words. The man's gaze ran down the length of him. Searching for injuries? Had Jonah been hurt in the fight?

A new line of dread wove through him. If he'd wounded this man's brother, his reception would be far worse than he'd hoped.

But Jericho offered a nod. "Come up to the house. The women are waiting."

Eric clamped his jaw as he leaned forward to dismount. He couldn't let Jericho see his pain. Any sign of weakness could be used against him.

Thankfully, the man turned to talk with Two Stones, and Eric made it to the ground. He pressed his hand against his ribs to lessen the fire inside, then turned to riffle through his pack. He couldn't forget the doll he'd brought for Mary Ellen.

He followed the others toward the barn, but it was all he could do to stay upright and take small breaths as he followed.

Jericho tied the horses to a rail in front of the barn, then they started up the slope. Eric had caught his breath finally, and the pain ebbed to the steady throb he'd endured during the ride.

Near the cabin, the scent of woodsmoke filled the air. Jericho opened the door and took the single step up to the building, moving inside as a rush of warmth swept out.

As Eric entered, his eyes had to adjust to the dimmer light. Then he found her.

Naomi stood near the center of the room with their daughter cradled in her arms—a vision of strength and beauty. Her gaze was fixed on him, though hard to read. Certainly not pleased to see him. Was she trying to hold in anger for the sake of their daughter?

Mary Ellen watched him with those same wide eyes, both curious and uncertain.

For a moment, silence hung with the weight of what had happened the day before, with the echoes of past promises and their current unsteady truce.

Finally, Naomi spoke, her voice steady, belying the tension displayed in the way she clung to their daughter. "You made it."

Eric cleared his throat, struggling to find his own voice. "Nothing could have stopped me."

Mary Ellen wriggled in her mother's arms. Was there recognition on her face? Or just the natural curiosity of a child toward a stranger? He could only hope those eyes would eventually light with pleasure when she saw him.

"Come sit." Naomi motioned toward the half-circle of chairs gathered around the hearth, where a small fire burned, the flames low.

He wanted to go straight to Naomi and Mary Ellen, but he should do as she wished. He had to start today off on a better track than yesterday.

So he stepped toward the chairs, and Naomi followed, settling into the rocker. He took the straight-backed seat beside her.

Two Stones and Heidi talked with Jericho and Dinah on the opposite side of the room, near a large table.

Eric kept his attention on the woman and child beside him, turning his chair a little so he could face them. "Hello." He focused on his daughter. "Do you remember me from yesterday?" As he spoke, memory slipped in of the crying he'd heard in the background after Jericho split up the fight. Mary Ellen was more likely to recall that debacle than the moments the two of them had shared when he'd first met her on the hillside.

The girl looked up at Naomi, and a few sounds babbled from her mouth, but no words he could decipher.

Naomi might have made sense of them though, for a gentle smile curved her mouth as she looked at the girl. "This is your papa." She pointed to Eric.

Eric's breath stalled. Had Mary Ellen *said* Papa? Surely he would have caught those sounds. Maybe Naomi was simply instructing.

Eric reached into his pocket and pulled out the doll, then held it up. "I brought you something. A friend." He'd had no idea what his daughter would look like, so he'd selected this wooden girl with hair made of yarn the color of cornsilk, closer to the dark blonde of Naomi's than the black-ish brown of the other figurines in the store. Maybe he could somehow replace the yellow yarn with something red and curly. He'd have to think about what that might be.

Interest flicked in Mary Ellen's eyes, and for a fleeting moment, a glimmer of warmth shone in Naomi's gaze as well. The tension in the air seemed to lessen a little.

The girl extended a tentative finger to touch the toy, brushing the yellow yarn hair. She drew back, her brows gathering.

What could he do to help her accept it? He'd never had a sister—no siblings at all. His cousin Harvey was the closest thing to a brother, but Eric had no experience with young girls.

Eric pitched his voice high and wiggled the doll as though she were speaking. "Hello. I'm looking for a friend. Will you be my friend?"

Mary Ellen curled into Naomi's shoulder, her hands coming up into fists to cover the smile that slipped out. They didn't hide the light in her eyes, though, so he pressed on in that same girlish tone. "I like your curly hair. It's so pretty and red. What's your name?"

Mary Ellen's smile broadened, and she shifted one of her fists away from her mouth. "Me-me."

His heart leaped at the sound of that sweet voice. That was how she'd said her name yesterday too.

He continued speaking through the doll. "It's a pleasure to meet you, Me-me. I don't have a name. Can you help me choose one? What can my name be?"

Mary Ellen's gaze lifted to him with uncertainty, as though considering whether it was him speaking or the doll. Then she extended her hand to touch the hair again. Or maybe to take the toy?

The pudgy hand paused before reaching the doll.

Eric spoke quieter so he didn't startle her, still using the high-pitched voice. "Will you hold me? I'd like to be your friend."

That seemed to be what Mary Ellen needed, for she grabbed the doll and cradled her against her shoulder, then wiggled her upper body in a rocking motion. She started babbling to the toy.

He smiled, watching his daughter make a new friend. She would be so much fun once she opened up to him. What a special daughter he had—remarkable inside and out.

His gaze slipped up to Naomi. She was watching Mary Ellen, which gave him a moment to study her. *She* was the main reason their daughter was so perfect. Not only did the girl possess part of her mother's nature and abilities, but Naomi had nurtured her all these months, teaching and encouraging her. And yes, protecting her.

Their daughter had grown into such a wonderful child mostly because of Naomi.

And maybe also with help from these other people. He owed them all a debt of gratitude. And he could start repaying them with a *thank you*.

Naomi must have felt his gaze, for hers lifted to meet his.

He worked to find the words, then started with the two most important. "Thank you."

Her brows gathered.

He pressed on. "You've done a remarkable job with her. With our daughter." Emotion clogged in his throat, and he paused and swallowed it down. "Thank you for everything. For caring for her. For letting me meet her." And so much more.

Naomi's eyes shone, but she didn't speak. Only nodded, then dropped her focus back to the girl.

That might have been partly because Mary Ellen was bouncing the toy up Naomi's arm, *walking* up to her shoulder. She wiggled it in Naomi's face, babbling nonsensical sounds. Clearly the doll was talking to Naomi.

Naomi leaned back a little as she spoke to the toy. "It's nice to meet you, Dolly."

Had Naomi understood the chatter? Had Mary Ellen really named the figure Dolly? Perhaps Naomi was simply playing along, selecting a name quickly that would work until Mary Ellen was old enough to choose one herself.

Either way, Naomi was clearly a remarkable mother.

He swallowed once more, clearing away more emotion from his throat. He'd dreamed of sitting with her, playing with their first child. He'd never ever imagined the moment would look like this.

CHAPTER 6

*N*aomi's nerves flipped as she approached the bunkhouse. Jonah hadn't come out yet today, though it was already midafternoon. When the rest of the men came to the main house for the morning meal, Jude said Jonah was still sleeping. She'd attempted to check on him after the breakfast dishes were done, but her knocks on the door were met with silence.

Surely he would be awake now. Maybe he'd stayed in the bunkhouse to avoid Eric.

She'd wondered if Eric would even come after Dinah's description of how she and Jericho had found him—laid on the side of a mountain with his horse not even unsaddled. She'd said he hadn't really awakened as she checked his abdomen, making sure there was no internal bleeding and confirming two ribs showed signs of being broken.

Naomi still couldn't believe they'd left him like that, but Dinah had been firm in her answer that they'd made certain he had no life-threatening injuries. Now they needed to let him make choices for himself. Good thing Two Stones and Heidi had found him and helped him reach the ranch. And convinced him to go on with them to stay in their Salish village. A good decision, since he would have a warm bark lodge to sleep in. Plenty of food and people around to care for him, especially with his injuries.

But he would be so far away. A two-hour ride. How often would he come to see Mary Ellen? He'd been thousands of miles away for the first ten months of the girl's life. Two hours was a vast improvement, but how often would he make the trip?

His visit that morning had gone far better than Naomi had let herself hope. He'd stayed for nearly two hours, sitting on the floor with their daughter, building with her blocks. They'd even constructed a makeshift house for the doll he brought her.

Then he'd read from the two books Jericho had ordered for her, an illustrated edition of *Aesop's Fables* and *Gammer Gurton's Garland*. Mary Ellen never seemed to understand or care about the words. But the brightly painted pictures in the former always caught her attention, at least for a half minute. Eric realized that quickly, and made up stories about each picture. Sometimes he would match the story to the written text, but more often than not, he made up a much wilder version. Naomi had never realized what an imagination he had.

He'd said he would return tomorrow, though he'd not said how long he would stay in the territory before he went back east. Months, she hoped.

She couldn't let herself wish for longer. She had pledged to marry Jonah, who would provide a wonderful home for her and Mary Ellen—a solid, stable life. He was such a good man.

She was lucky he'd asked her. Fortunate he was willing to build such a wonderful cabin for them.

A cabin just as large as Jericho and Dinah's, with two separate bed chambers and a loft above them. She would have her own bed chamber if she wanted, which she would likely share with Mary Ellen, as she did now. She'd have her own kitchen. Her own...everything. And she'd have Jonah there with her—a good friend and partner. He'd said he wouldn't push her for any marital rights. Those would be available if she wanted them, but he held no expectations.

How could she not want the picture he painted? And it wasn't an idle dream, as Eric's had been back when he'd offered her marriage. Jonah was actually building this cabin. It was why he'd gone to Fort Benton, to pick up real windows. He would, no doubt, be cutting more logs today if he weren't injured.

She stood at the bunkhouse door. Had Eric's presence and the fight ruined it all? Surely she could make Jonah see she didn't care about Eric. Well...not in the way she once had.

She pushed aside the niggling voice that questioned the truth of that thought and knocked softly on the door. "Jonah?" She strained to hear any rustling or movement inside. Was that a footstep?

The latch clicked, then the door creaked open, revealing Jonah's tired face. The shadows under his eyes seemed darker than usual, the crook in his nose quite pronounced. Dinah had not exaggerated his injuries.

She offered a tentative smile. "Hello."

He leaned against the door frame, the strain in his expression softening as his gaze roamed her face. "Hey." His voice was roughened, from sleep or disuse she couldn't tell. There was a vulnerability in his gaze, and maybe a touch of relief.

"I was worried about you. Are you...in pain?" That was a silly question, both because he surely hurt all over, especially his nose, and also because she had no doubt Jonah would his aches, as all the men around here tended to do. Too hard-headed for their own good sometimes.

He shook his head—as she'd expected—but then stepped aside to allow her into the bunkhouse's dim interior. "I've just been thinking a lot. There's something I want to tell you."

She knew better than to enter a man's room. That had been her mistake with Harvey—not his room of course, but she'd entered the house when he was the only one there, lured in by his promise of news about Eric—and she'd paid dearly for the error.

So no, she couldn't step inside this bunkhouse. Not that she mistrusted Jonah...quite the opposite. But that experience had left its mark, both on her heart and her body.

Jonah seemed to realize her discomfort, for his expression turned stricken. "Of course. I'm sorry." He stepped into the doorway. "I wasn't thinking. Let's go up to the house." He motioned for her to precede him.

As they started up the hill, the tension between them stretched like an invisible thread. She glanced his way, noting the determined set of his jaw. The sight of him, bruised but unbroken, fanned a spark of something warm in her chest.

"How did things go with Eric?" His tone was gentle, empty of the jealousy she'd seen in his eyes after the fight yesterday. Maybe he'd worked through whatever uncertainties had troubled him.

A bit of pressure eased from her chest. "All went well. Mary Ellen was shy at first, but Eric gave her a doll. They played for a while, then he left with Two Stones and Heidi. I guess he'll be staying with them."

"That's good. He stayed quite a while." Jonah must have been watching. He kept his focus on the ground now. "I guess he's doing what he can to get to know her."

Was Jonah also thinking *and you*? She needed to set his mind at ease there.

She inhaled a breath of the cold air. "I'm glad for that. It's good for her to know her father." Then she looked at Jonah, slowing her walk, hoping he'd meet her gaze. He didn't, but she had to say this part anyway. "Jonah, him being here won't change what you and I have. Eric is Mary Ellen's father and part of my past. But *you* are my future." She managed a smile. "A future I'm looking forward to."

Jonah stopped and studied her. She did her best to show earnestness in her eyes. She couldn't lose this man. She had to make him see she was committed.

At last, his expression eased. "I'm glad."

Yet there was still a tension that made him look tired, older than his years. His gaze shifted to the ground, and he toed the dirt around a rock. "I should apologize for getting into it with him. I just..." He scrubbed a hand through his hair, then looked up at her, and finally she could see the real Jonah in his eyes. The earnest care he didn't show many people. "I was afraid I might be losing the you—you and Mary Ellen. That scared me more than anything has in a long time. You're important to me. Both of you."

Her insides twisted, emotion welling into her throat and burning her eyes. How long had she wanted a man to say those words to her? Jonah truly was everything she wanted in a man. Everything she *needed*. A solid presence. Security. A man willing to put her needs before his own. A man who wouldn't disappear without responding to her letters.

Jonah was different. He was exactly who she needed.

She reached for him, sliding her fingers down his arm to his hand, fitting her palm against his. Then she managed a few important words. "Thank you. That means...everything."

His mouth curved into a smile, the corners of his eyes crinkling with affection. But as quickly as it appeared, the smile vanished, replaced by a wince of pain that made her own heart ache in sympathy.

"Your nose hurts, doesn't it? I'm sorry you had to suffer for my sake."

He waved off her words. "It's nothing I can't handle. You and Mary Ellen are worth it."

Such kindness. Such selflessness. He deserved a special reaction from her. She wasn't ready to offer a kiss, but maybe a hug of thanks would suffice.

She sent a quick glance to gauge his expression but didn't let herself linger in thinking about it. Just stepped forward and wrapped her arms around his waist.

He pulled her close, slipping his hands around her, holding her tight in the crib of his security. He smelled good, like leather and lye soap and something else entirely masculine.

She didn't stay long. She couldn't allow him to think she wanted more than this. But when she pulled back, she smiled. "Thank you."

He gave a solid nod, then continued up the hill. "We'd better get inside before it turns any colder."

When they reached the cabin, he opened the door for her. She stepped into the cozy warmth of the house, the rich scent of baking bread and wood smoke enveloping her. Her gaze landed on the seating around the fire, that straight-backed chair Eric had sat in when he offered the doll to their daughter.

"Oh-na!" Mary Ellen's squeal broke through her thoughts.

A glance toward the kitchen showed Dinah wrestling with the squirming girl. "Hang on there, sweet one. Let me set you down."

The moment Mary Ellen's feet touched the floor, she toddled toward Naomi, doll clutched in her hand. But she passed right by her mother.

Jonah scooped her up, lifting her to eye level. "Hey there, Cricket. What's that you have?"

Instead of holding up Dolly, Mary Ellen studied Jonah's face, concern forming a line between her brows.

She reached out a finger and touched his nose.

He winced, then grabbed the pudgy digit and brought it to his mouth to land a loud kiss on the tip. "I'll take that finger. In fact, I think I'll eat it." He sounded like a hungry bear as he pretended to munch down the length of her finger, then over her hand and up her arm.

Mary Ellen convulsed into a fit of giggles as she tried to pull away from Jonah's tickling mouth.

He paused for air, and his face looked a little paler, the shadows under his eyes darkening. Had he bumped his nose?

He didn't continue the antics but kept Mary Ellen in his arms as he turned to speak to Dinah.

Naomi soaked in the sight of them. Her soon-to-be-husband, strong and capable and so relaxed with her daughter in his arms.

She'd made the right decision.

Hadn't she?

If only she could kill the longing that still pressed deep inside. Eric was her past. She had to make sure Jonah remained her future.

CHAPTER 7

*E*ric's body might have frozen in this hunched position, so long they'd been riding in the biting wind. This was the only posture he'd found that kept the pain in his ribs to a dull throb. Surely they were almost to Two Stones's village.

He rode beside Running Woman, Two Stones's mother. Two Stones and Heidi—Mrs. Two Stones, but she'd insisted he call her by her Christian name—led their group, and Two Stones's elderly father, White Bear, brought up the rear.

The damp chill in the air might mean rain. Though the biting wind felt cold, the atmosphere didn't seem quite cold enough for snow.

For that he was thankful. He'd arranged with Jericho to return tomorrow for another couple of hours with his daughter. He'd been doing his best to commit the trail to memory—focusing on landmarks. Boulders that formed unusual shapes. Trees with distinctive branches reaching out like the arms of a clock at ten to two. A snowfall could change the landscape entirely. The last thing he needed was to get lost in a snow-covered mountain wilderness.

Beside him, Running Woman's horse snorted, the sound

sharp in the quiet. The older woman turned her weathered face toward him, her eyes taking him in with a friendliness that reminded him of his Grandma LaGrange.

He'd never thought his allies on this journey would be a native family, but he was grateful.

As the land leveled out some, Heidi turned back to him, her expression sympathetic. "We're almost there. You can rest soon."

He nodded. "I'm fine." Did he wear his pain so openly?

Dinah had insisted on checking him for injuries, and she'd confirmed two of his ribs were broken. Thankfully, no internal organs had been punctured. She recommended he take Two Stones up on his offer of shelter in their village, but a hint of worry had touched her eyes. *Be careful as you ride back and forth,* she'd said. *Keep your horse to a walk and try to sit as still as you can. Your ribs won't heal as quickly if you move around too much.*

How could he not shift about as he rode up and down these mountains? He wouldn't delay time with his daughter for a couple of broken bones. If travel proved too hard, he would camp near the ranch.

The trees thinned, and what must be the village came into view. In the valley stood a collection of round structures, some wooden and some made of leather. The homes were lined in neat rows, though the sizes varied. Two Stones and Heidi led their group toward the right end of the village.

They halted at a larger wooden home near the edge of the grouping, and Two Stones slid to the ground. As he moved to Heidi's horse to help her, he glanced back at Eric. "This is the home of my mother and father. It is bigger than the one Heidi and I share. You will be comfortable here."

"Thank you." Eric kept one hand bracing his ribs as he eased from his horse. As long as he could lie down soon, he'd make do anywhere.

Running Woman had already dismounted. She left her animal and motioned for Eric to follow her. He should untie his blankets and packs before going in so he wouldn't have to come back for them. And he would need to see to his horse.

The thought sent a fresh shot of pain through his middle. When Running Woman motioned to him again, he followed. He'd do what needed to be done after he rested.

Though the afternoon sun was bright outside, within, the hut was dim. The only light filtered in through a chimney opening in the center of the roof and through the doorway.

She motioned to the far left side of the room. "Lay."

He moved that direction, and as his eyes adjusted to the light, he could make out a stack of furs. The pile looked plenty long enough for him to stretch out. He really should see to his horse and belongings first, but Running Woman urged him forward, hands on her hips like a mother with an unruly lad.

He was not strong enough to fight her. Not that he particularly wanted to.

He dropped to his knees on the furs, then turned to lower onto his side. He was becoming adept at the specific way to move to keep his ribs from screaming out. Someday, he'd like to be able to inhale a deep breath again, but for now, he'd settle for lying flat and closing his eyes so he could just...be...still.

* * *

*C*risp morning air filled the small cabin as Naomi stood by the window, her breath fogging the glass. Down at the barn, the men were all riding out in different directions. Jericho, Gil, and Sampson would work with the herd in the south pasture. Jonah and Miles planned to install windows in Jonah's cabin today, and Jude was taking Angela for a ride around the ranch. Those two were so sweet together, both of them quiet amid the clamor of voices when the entire group sat at the dining table. Love hummed between them anytime they looked at each other....or simply stood in the same room.

As the two rode side by side toward the trail leading to the east pasture, Naomi's chest ached. She remembered feeling like that with Eric. It had seemed impossible that anything could separate them—ever.

"I don't know why we have to do this." Sean's voice grumbled from behind her. "We've been gone more than a month. Jonah needs me at the cabin."

Weariness pressed on her as she turned to face her charges.

Lillian and Sean sat at the large table that served as their classroom during the day, books and slates laid out before them. This wouldn't be an easy morning. After they took a break from schooling, as they had while the two traveled to Fort Benton with the others, Sean was always restless. What seven-year-old boy wouldn't be?

But they had to get back at it. Naomi committed to teaching these two as if they attended a regular school. This was her primary job here on the ranch, this and keeping up with cooking and cleaning. And her daughter.

She slid a glance at Mary Ellen where she played on the rug with the abacus they used for arithmetic. The girl pushed aside the tool and crawled to the crates they'd stacked in front of the cold hearth. Soon, they would need more than the cookstove to keep the cabin warm, but until then, they'd placed this barrier to keep Mary Ellen from hurting herself on the raised stone or getting dirty in the soot.

Just now though, Mary Ellen was scooting the top crate over, nearly pushing it off the stack as she aimed for the fireplace behind.

Naomi strode toward her. "No, you don't." She scooped up her daughter and nudged the box back in place.

Mary Ellen shrieked, pressing against Naomi's shoulder as she vented her anger and frustration.

Naomi carried her daughter to the table. "Sit next to Lillian. You can draw on your slate like she is."

Naomi settled the girl in the chair, and Lillian handed her a piece of chalk. "Look. You can draw a horse." Lillian was so good with her, a natural mother, even at twelve years old.

Mary Ellen's protests dwindled into sniffling as she took the chalk Lillian offered, her small fingers fumbling until she found a firm hold.

"Horsie." Lillian repeated, earning a grin from her young cousin.

Naomi watched, letting that smile soothe her spirit. Then she turned back to Sean and forced a pleasant expression as she sat next to him. "The sooner we finish our studies, the sooner you can go help Uncle Jonah. And you're learning things that will help in the work. Multiplication will be useful your entire life, no matter what you do. Building a cabin, calculating food needed for the animals through the winter, and even helping at the mine, estimating profit per crate." Perhaps she should give examples of life outside the ranch, but the boy seemed to love every part of this place. In truth, she understood the feeling. This ranch had become a haven to her. Why would she ever want to leave?

Sean scowled at the arithmetic book before him, his freckled nose wrinkling, but he knew better than to complain again. A blonde curl flopped over his forehead as he focused, but Naomi kept herself from brushing it back with the rest of his waves. Both siblings had beautiful pale blond hair, but Lillian's was as straight as a broom stick.

A soft knock on the door drew their attention, and Sean jumped to his feet, nearly sending his chair tumbling.

Naomi's heart sprinted. Could Eric be here already? They'd not clearly defined the time for him to come, but she'd assumed it would be closer to noon, like yesterday. Especially since he was staying so far away.

Yet no one else would knock. Except...maybe Angela? Had she and Jude returned for something they forgot?

Naomi followed Sean as he jerked the door open enough to peer through. After looking at the newcomer, he sent her an uncertain glance, which made her insides tighten all the more. He wouldn't hesitate if it was Angela.

Sean opened the door all the way, and Eric stood outside.

The sight of him made her heart stutter from something very different than nerves. Those perfect features, the dark auburn hair, just long enough to form loose curls. And those eyes...his devastating eyes were looking at her almost the way he had back when they'd first been courting.

A rush of emotions sent a tremor through Naomi's body. There was so much history in that gaze, so much left unsaid between them.

But Lillian and Sean were watching. She couldn't let anyone see how much Eric's presence affected her. She nodded. "Eric."

The corners of his lips lifted slightly, that familiar half-smile that used to disarm all her defenses. "I hope I'm not too early. The ride went faster than I anticipated."

She shook her head, unable to find more words as Sean stepped aside to let him in.

As Eric crossed the threshold, the lad eyed him suspiciously before retreating to his seat.

Eric's gaze stayed locked on her.

Naomi's cheeks warmed under his scrutiny, but she managed a tight smile. "You're just in time for arithmetic lessons."

He finally shifted his focus to the table. A flicker of surprise crossed his face, maybe from seeing Mary Ellen sitting with the older two?

Eric sent Naomi a quick look, his eyes asking permission.

She gave a small nod, and he stepped to the table. "Hello, Master Sean. Miss Lillian. I see you're both hard at work."

He didn't stop until he reached Mary Ellen, who had stood

on her seat and gripped the back as he approached. "Hello, princess."

Instead of reaching for her, he bent low so he could peer at her over the back. The child studied him, only her eyes peeking above the wood. She looked more mischievous than shy this time. Hopefully she remembered him from yesterday.

Eric clamped a hand over his eyes, paused for two heart-beats, then lowered it quickly. "Peek-a-boo."

He earned the hint of a smile playing at the corners of Mary Ellen's mouth.

When he repeated the action, her mirth blossomed into a wide grin that sparkled in her eyes. "Mo!" She bounced like she always did when she was excited.

Eric obliged, playing the game again and finally earning a giggle.

Oh, that laugh... It stirred something deep inside Naomi, a pleasure that raised its head so rarely.

As he repeated the game a few more times, Mary Ellen's infectious giggles filled the room, mixing with Eric's deeper chuckle. At last, he straightened and tweaked her nose. "You're a lot of fun."

He turned to Lillian and Sean with a friendly grin, peering over their shoulders to the books and slates on the table. "Stud-ies, I see. What are you working on?"

Lillian's voice was shy as she nudged her book. "I'm reading, and Sean is working sums."

Eric looked like he wanted to ask more questions, but Mary Ellen made a grab for him, and he barely caught her before she toppled off the chair. "Whoa, there, princess." He lifted her into his arms, and flash of pain in his eyes showed his ribs still had much healing to do. Yet his expression changed to pleasure as he pulled their daughter close. Seeing them together like that— the two people she loved the most so happy—brought a rise of heat to Naomi's eyes that she had to blink away.

She returned to her chair and settled in beside Sean. Might as well give Eric time with his daughter. "Now, let's say those multiplication tables again."

Sean was mid-sigh when the door opened and Dinah entered, carrying a crate of medical supplies. She smiled at them all as she came to the table and set the box down with a soft thud.

"Hello." Her gaze scanned the scene before her, lingering on Eric. "Good morning, Eric. We didn't expect you so early."

He smiled at Dinah, shifting only his eyes since Mary Ellen was patting his beard. "The ride went faster than I expected."

"Well." She patted the box. "Is it all right if I sort these supplies here? The new bandages have to be refolded."

Frustration pressed in Naomi's chest. How in the world was she to re-establish any sort of order in the children's studies with all these distractions?

Before Naomi could manage a polite response, Sean asked, "Can we go out and use the logs for multiplication like we did before?"

That sounded so appealing. Away from these interferences. Away from the draw of Eric's presence. They could bring their workbooks, and she could adjust the assignments to use the real objects around them.

But did she dare leave the babe with Eric?

"That's a good idea." Dinah probably read her thoughts. "Eric and I can stay here with Mary Ellen. You three enjoy being outside before it gets too cold to do so."

Naomi met her sister's gaze, and Dinah gave a nod of silent confirmation. She would make sure all went well here.

When she glanced at Eric, he also dipped his chin. "I'll be here with Mary Ellen until you come back. I'm sure Dinah can help me if we need anything."

That had to suffice. She nodded, turning to Sean and Lillian.

"Very well. Bring your books and coats. And your slates and chalk too."

The boy nearly sprinted to the door, and even Lillian looked relieved as she gathered her items and followed her brother.

Naomi allowed one more look at her sister and Eric, but the former had already begun pulling folded cloth from the crate, and the latter was talking to Mary Ellen as she held up her doll.

All would be well here. Surely.

CHAPTER 8

$\mathcal{N}$aomi jogged to catch up with Lillian, then slowed to walk beside her while Sean ran ahead. As they moved into the path through the woods, he leapt up to pull pine needles from the trees every few steps. At least he was using up all that extra energy.

The clearing where Jonah was building their cabin was less than five minutes' walk from the main house, and she could hear Jonah and Miles talking even before the structure came into view through the trees.

Her heart quickened at the thought of seeing Jonah. He would get that glimmer of happy pride in his eyes as he told her what they were working on. That hint of longing for the day they would finally be able to move in there as man and wife. They'd not shared much physical contact, not even a kiss. Sometimes he brushed her arm in passing, and their hands grazed when they passed Mary Ellen between them. But he'd given her space, allowing her to adjust to the idea of their coming marriage.

She was eager to have her own home. And Jonah would be a good husband.

But...

Her middle always knotted when he gave her that look. It was as if marrying her and building the cabin would be the culmination of all his dreams.

Hers too. Except a few details that hadn't seemed important until Eric showed up.

She and Lillian stepped into the clearing, and the half-built cabin stood before them. The walls rose up to waist-height. Jonah and Miles were working a two-man saw through the top log to the right of the opening that would hold the door, cutting out the opening for a window, she guessed.

Jonah's back was too them, and Miles must have been too focused to notice their approach. She allowed a quick look at Jonah as he bent, straining to pull the saw through the sappy pine. Life on the ranch had given him a strong, muscled form. Plenty strong enough to keep her and Mary Ellen safe and cared for. And he had those Coulter good looks, an added benefit.

She moved her gaze to the cabin itself, her mind filling in the remaining structure. She would have curtains framing the windows, and she would plant wildflowers on either side of the door. To the right of the house was a fairly level area where she could put a vegetable garden. The growing season wouldn't be long here, but how wonderful it would feel to work with the plants while the sun shone warm overhead.

Sean shouted something that caught the men's attention. The paused their sawing, and when Jonah turned and saw her, the easy smile he sent sank through her, warm like a hearth fire on a winter's eve. He wiped his brow with his forearm, then walked toward them. Sean trotted inside the cabin walls, only his bobbing head visible as he aimed toward his Uncle Miles.

"Didn't expect to see you here this morning." Jonah's pleasure took on that look of hopeful longing that made her want to step back.

But she forced a bright expression. "We thought a change of

scenery might help us get back into the rhythm of studies." She glanced past Jonah to where Sean was scampering along the front of the cabin to the place Jonah had been standing. Maybe Miles was allowing him to try his hand at being the other man to wield the saw. "It's nice to see the progress."

Jonah turned to eye the building. "It's coming along. We'll have it finished and ready before Christmas if we keep at it."

She nodded, the weight of those words settling in her gut. Ready for Christmas. Ready for a life she had agreed to but was now seeming much less desirable than before.

"Sean is supposed to use the logs to practice his multiplication tables." Lillian's voice held that big-sister tone, the one proving she wanted to make sure her little brother didn't have too much fun.

Jonah eyed her. "Sounds like the best way to learn. I'd be grateful if you both can figure out how many more logs and nails we need to finish these walls."

Naomi smiled. "That's a fine way to put their lessons to practical use." She touched Lillian's shoulder. "Let's go pull your brother away from that saw before he hurts himself."

Sean had taken up Jonah's end and was heaving the blade back and forth with his entire body. Miles manned the other side, likely bearing the brunt of the work. But Sean appeared to be doing as much of his part as an eight-year-old boy could.

She started toward them, a niggle of worry slipping in as Sean strained to pull the saw back at an odd angle. The leg he braced himself with was far too close to the saw blade, or at least it appeared so from this distance.

She called out, "Be careful, Sean."

He glanced back at her as he pushed the saw handle toward Miles. His teeth flashed white in a grin, showing just how much he loved working with his uncles.

When he pulled the blade back with a heave, his foot slipped out from beneath him. His upper body dropped as his legs flew into the air.

He yelped, and Naomi's heart slammed. Had he hurt himself? She couldn't tell if his legs had struck the blade or not.

She sprinted forward. She couldn't see him well through the tall wheatgrass between them.

Then a howl rose up that made her heart nearly cease beating. "Sean!"

He lay curled on the ground, clutching the top of his thigh as blood spilled through his fingers. *Lord, don't let him have cut an artery.*

Jonah had nearly bled to death when his thigh bone broke in an accident that had happened the day she and Dinah arrived at the ranch. They couldn't lose Sean from a leg injury. And under her care.

Jonah reached him first, kneeling at his side. She dropped next to him. "What's hurt?"

Sean's howls had turned to sobs, and no wonder. Blood covered both his hands. Jonah was trying to pry one of them away to see the injury.

They had to slow the bleeding.

She glanced around for something to tie around his leg. A rope. A piece of cloth. Anything long enough.

Her gaze snagged on Jonah's shirt pocket. "Your handkerchief." She didn't wait for him to hand it over, just yanked the cloth out.

The white square she'd stitched for him wouldn't be long enough, though. Her chest squeezed as she threw the cloth down. "Rope. I need something to tie around his leg to slow the bleeding."

Jonah was holding his hands over Sean's now, helping cover the wound and maybe keep some of the blood inside.

"Here." Miles yanked his leather braces off his shoulders, then thrust them toward her. Perfect.

She quickly worked them under the boy's leg. She knew enough for this part, but they needed Dinah. Now.

"Go for my sister." She spoke as she worked. "Tell her it's urgent."

Miles answered. "Lillian's already gone."

Jonah was murmuring over Sean's quieter sobs, fully focused on putting pressure on the wound and encouraging the boy.

She pulled the knot in the leather strap, then checked to see how snug it fit around Sean's leg. Hopefully that was right. It felt impossibly tight, but it might not even be enough. She'd never been trained in these things like Dinah had. Maybe she should have spent more time with Pop in the clinic, learning from him along with her sister. Though she wasn't squeamish, she'd never been drawn to the sick and injured like her sister.

She eyed the mass of red covering Sean and Jonah's hands. Hers too. And Sean's trousers. And the ground around them.

Don't let him bleed out. You can't let him die. Please.

Was there something else she could do? She scanned the length of his body, but her mind was numb.

She rested her hand on Sean's shoulder. She'd like to brush the hair from his eyes, but then she'd smear blood on his face. "It's going to be all right, Sean. I know it hurts, but Dinah's almost here. You're going to be all right."

If only she could be certain her words were true.

* * *

*W*hen the cabin door burst open, Eric tightened his grip on his daughter as she spun to the source of the noise. They must have arrived with Sean.

Naomi charged inside, scurrying straight to one of the back rooms. Jonah and Miles came next, balancing Sean between them on a blanket, with Dinah at the boy's side. Lillian followed, clutching her hands together as worry twisted her features.

Mary Ellen must have sensed the tension, for she curled into Eric, pressing on his injured ribs.

He ignored the burning and wrapped his arms around her, letting her feel the safety in his hold. "It's all right, princess. Everything's all right."

When Lillian had burst in a quarter hour before saying her brother had been cut with the saw, Dinah had leapt into action. As she grabbed her medical bag and a blanket from one of the chairs, he'd asked what he could do to help.

Stay with Mary Ellen, had been her response. So he and his daughter had remained here on the rug, reading "The Tortoise and the Hare" for the twentieth time. His version of it at least. He'd have to buy her more books when he could get to town.

Just now though, they had far more important things to worry about.

The group disappeared into the room Naomi had entered, but their voices drifted easily through the open doorway.

"Lay him here," Dinah instructed. "Gently now."

"It's all right, Sean." That was one of the brothers. "You're going to be just fine."

Was he? Eric needed to see for himself. The only glimpse he'd gotten had revealed blood everywhere. And his quiet sobs now, so long after the injury happened, meant he must still be in great pain.

Eric patted the floor beside him. "Can you stand here a minute?" Getting up would be hard enough with his ribs, but nearly impossible with Mary Ellen in his arms.

After struggling to his feet, Eric kept one hand over his middle until the fire eased. He took a cautious step forward, peering into the room where they'd taken Sean.

It was a bed chamber, and the boy lay in a narrow bunk. Dinah was working quickly, her manner the focused efficiency of a doctor.

Naomi stood beside her, accepting bloodied cloths and handing over the things Dinah asked for.

The men and the girl stood back a little, blocking Eric's view of the injury.

He could see Naomi's face, though, and she might have felt his gaze, for she glanced his way.

The sorrow in her eyes made his chest clench. If only he could stride in there and help. What could he do though? Dinah was right that he could bring the most benefit by keeping Mary Ellen occupied. The girl pressed into his leg now, clutching Dolly as she studied the group around Sean.

He rested his hand on his daughter's head. "Here, princess. Let's go back and finish our book." He would sit in a chair this time so he could get up easier if there was an opportunity to help.

A few minutes after he'd settled with his daughter in his lap and the book open before them, Jonah and Miles stepped from the room, their faces lined with exhaustion.

Jonah's gaze flicked to Eric, his eyes wary.

Eric held his tongue. The last thing he wanted was to say something to raise the man's ire during this tense time.

Did he dare ask about Miles's condition?

Jonah turned away, barking orders to his younger brother. "Get two buckets of clean water. I'm sure they'll need it for Sean. Maybe three. I'll fill the wood box."

They strode outside, leaving the room quiet once more. He tried to focus on the book and his daughter, but the murmur of women's voices made him strain to try to make out their words. They were too soft to understand.

By the time, the men had each made two trips inside with their respective loads, Lillian stepped from the bed chamber.

Eric could sit still no longer, so he eased his daughter to the floor and pushed to his feet. Rising from the chair was far easier than from the floor, no question about it.

"How is he?" Jonah spoke Eric's question before he could, and they all studied the Lillian's face as she moved into the kitchen area and pulled a big pot from a lower shelf, which she placed on the cookstove.

"Dinah says it didn't cut the main artery, just a smaller one. But he lost a lot of blood. I'm making soup to help rebuild his strength." She sounded so determined. Like a grown woman, not a girl of twelve or thirteen.

Her own brother was the one suffering in there, yet she hadn't collapsed on the floor in a fit of sobs. She was out here cooking, doing what she could to help.

Eric stepped closer, moving around the others to reach the stove. "What can I do? I'm a deft hand at chopping vegetables."

She didn't spare him a look but pulled a sack from a crate and plopped it on the counter. "Cut these potatoes into the pot. Thin slices. Make sure you cut off the eyes."

Cut off the eyes? He'd been stretching the truth a little with the words *deft hand*, but surely he could manage to slice a few potatoes. ...and cut off their eyes, whatever that meant.

When he pulled the first spud from the bag, a memory slipped in. Their cook back in Charleston—where his family had lived until they moved to Wayneston when he was fifteen— had let him watch her work sometimes. She'd talked about how potatoes were actually seeds and would sprout if left too long before being eaten. She'd called these sprouts eyes, if he remembered right.

He worked slowly with the first potato, making sure he cut out the roots of each sprout, then making small slices into the pot.

Lillian moved far faster, chopping radishes and carrots.

"Hmm," he murmured. "I'd better step up my pace if I want to keep my job."

She didn't look at him, but he caught a corner of her mouth

ticking up. Maybe that was the best he'd get, all things considered.

In the living area, Jonah had scooped up Mary Ellen and was talking with her quietly. Perhaps Eric should have stayed with his daughter, doing what he'd been told. But he'd felt like Lillian needed someone with her just now.

And as he slid glances at Coulter and Mary Ellen, he couldn't deny how well the two seemed to know each other. How comfortable they were with each other. Coulter pretended to steal Mary Ellen's nose, but when he asked her where it was, she shook her head. Then he tickled her belly, and she convulsed in a fit of giggles.

That laughter. Eric would never ever grow tired of the sound, no matter how much he heard it. The fact that Jonah was the cause this time niggled in his chest, but at least his daughter was finding joy. The merriment lightened the tension in the room too. Even Lillian cast a half-smile toward the pair.

A savory aroma was already beginning to waft from the bubbling concoction in the pot, making his middle gnaw. The Coulters surely wouldn't allow him to stay all day, but he'd be here as long as he could be useful. Perhaps they'd share a few bites of this stew. It certainly looked like enough to feed the entire Coulter clan.

Which he wasn't a part of. Nor did he wish to be.

He had the business he and his father had worked so hard to build back in Washington. He would only be here until the river thawed next spring, and by then he'd either have worked out a safe place for his child to thrive here, or he'd be taking her back home with him.

Today's injury had confirmed something he'd already know —this mountain country could be treacherous. It was not a safe place for a young girl to grow up.

Especially not his own daughter.

CHAPTER 9

The next day, Naomi's middle tightened as she allowed one more glance out the window. The lone figure she'd been waiting for finally appeared through the glass.

Eric rode his gelding to the hitching post at the barn, slipped down, and led the horse inside.

She turned to the room's occupants and forced a smile through her nerves. "He's here. Lillian, we'd best wear coats. I think the wind is cold today."

Lillian nodded, her own smile a touch apprehensive. "Come, Mary Ellen. I'll help you put your coat on."

Naomi moved to the crate she'd packed with food and a blanket. Eric had wanted to take Mary Ellen out of the cabin today, to picnic in a grassy field. She had hesitated to let them go alone. He didn't know the area, so he wouldn't know how to find the clearings where the grass grew abundantly. When she'd asked to go, he agreed amiably. She'd quickly dragged Lillian into the scheme, for the last thing she needed was to be alone with Eric, and little Mary Ellen wouldn't serve as a very good chaperone.

Poor Sean hadn't been cleared by Dr. Dinah to leave the

cabin except to visit the privy. He sat now at the table, his leg propped on a chair, with Angela across from him and the chess board between them. Sean had been the reigning champion of chess for months now, but it appeared he'd finally found his match in Angela.

Naomi riffled through the contents of the crate. Was she missing anything? She had serviettes to wipe their hands on, a knife to cut the cheese, spoons to scoop the pickled beets. A flask of warm chocolate—a special treat they rarely indulged in —along with cups for each of them. She'd even packed a dried apple pie she'd made the night before. Of course she'd baked made more for the family. These Coulters could put away dried apple pie like they inhaled it.

A knock sounded on the door, and Dinah stepped from her bed chamber, striding toward the front. "I'll get it."

Naomi turned to watch as Dinah lifted the latch and opened the door wide. "Come in." She motioned for Eric to enter. "I think the girls are ready."

Naomi should be doing something other than standing there when Eric entered, but she couldn't make herself move. Why did the thought of a picnic with Eric have her so addled?

He stepped in, then shifted so Dinah could close the door. His gaze found Naomi first, catching her staring at him. She tried for a smile. "I think we're ready."

He nodded. Had she said the same thing as Dinah? She had. Why was she being so ninny-headed?

Thankfully, Eric shifted his focus away from her, giving her space to think clearly again. Mostly. Good thing Jonah wasn't here to witness her daftness.

As he greeted Mary Ellen and Lillian, then moved to the table to speak with Sean and Angela, she grabbed her coat from the hook in her room and worked the buttons. She should carry the food crate so Eric didn't hurt his ribs.

She scooped it up and scanned the room. "We're ready."

"I'll carry that." Eric moved toward her, his hands outstretched.

She shook her head and strode to the door. "You're supposed to rest your ribs. Dinah, we'll be in that clearing on the way to the north pasture if you need us."

Dinah's voice followed her from behind. "Have fun and be careful."

She shifted the crate to one hip to open the door, then stepped out into the crisp breeze. She paused a moment to breathe in, letting the pure, bracing air fill her lungs. Many of the colorful leaves had fallen, leaving only a few brown ones amidst the evergreens.

Down at the corral, the new mare paced. She wanted freedom so desperately, but Jericho was worried about a leg injury that hadn't fully healed. Could the wound heal while the animal paced so much? Maybe the horse would settle if she were turned out in the herd.

But she also might squabble with the others, which could cause more damage. At least, that was Jericho's concern. He wanted to give the mare the best chance possible.

And truly...wouldn't it be wonderful if they all had someone like Jericho as an ally? Someone who had both the power to place them where they needed to be and also the care to ensure they were given every advantage to succeed?

Her chest tightened as the parallel to God came clear. Yet why did it feel like His path for her always had to be painful? She'd experienced enough of that already. Maybe what she'd done with Eric had been her own wayward step. But Harvey... She'd never invited his attention. She'd tried to stop him.

Her heart plunged into that racing pulse that always came when she thought of Eric's cousin. She inhaled a deep breath to pull herself out of that dark place. She stared up into the sky, a wide clear blue today, not a cloud in sight.

Eric, Lillian, and Mary Ellen had gathered behind her, and

she summoned a smile as she turned to face them. "Are we ready?"

Mary Ellen toddled forward, but Eric had a tight grip on her hand so she couldn't run down the hill. Naomi started toward the side of the cabin, aiming at the trees beyond. Better get her daughter moving so she could use that energy as long as she could manage.

The clearing wasn't far, a mere ten-minute walk from the cabin, but with Mary Ellen's small, eager steps, it took them nearly double that time. Naomi felt each second, measured in her daughter's delighted discoveries of every pebble and pinecone along the way. The tension inside her eased a little with Mary Ellen's babbling sounds.

Eric and Lillian walked on either side of her, exclaiming over each of her delighted discoveries.

At last, they stepped into the open area, a space about the size of three cabins. It felt secluded, surrounded by trees. She came here anytime she needed space to be alone, to uncluttter her mind, though she hadn't done so in a while.

Maybe she should have. Perhaps she'd have found more peace during the turmoil of these last weeks. It had started when Jonah asked her to marry him.

Or maybe before? How long exactly had this unrest churned inside her? In truth, she couldn't remember a time without it. Maybe back before Eric left, then didn't respond to her letters. Then Harvey. Then she found out she was with child, and she'd thought it was Harvey's.

When Mary Ellen had been born three weeks before she'd been expected, born with Eric's red curls, Naomi had finally allowed herself to hope. And believe. This babe wasn't the result of the man who'd forced himself on her. She was the outcome of two people who'd loved each other with every part of themselves. At least back then. They'd pushed that love much farther than they should have. But still, it had been love, not violence.

She set the crate down in the grass.

"This is nice." Eric scanned the area, then turned to her with a pleased smile. "I'll help set things out."

He unfolded the blanket and spread it over the ground. She would have shaken it out and let it flutter to the grass, but he worked methodically, opening the cover one fold at a time. Interesting how two people could go about things so differently yet accomplish the same goal.

She'd forgotten how careful and detailed Eric was when he worked. She'd always loved that about him. He was precise. That probably made him excellent with the deals he coordinated for his father's business.

While Lillian coaxed Mary Ellen into emptying her skirt full of treasures in a pile beside the blanket, Naomi pulled the food containers out of the crate.

They worked in silence. She handed plates and utensils to Eric to set out for each of them, then poured the chocolate.

"That smells so good I could feast on the drink alone." A grin played at Eric's mouth.

Naomi returned the smile as she handed him A steaming cup. "I've learned a new recipe. This one tops the way I made chocolate before, without question."

He raised his brows. "I'm intrigued. Your warm chocolate has always been my favorite. What makes this different?"

She gave him a sideways look. "A secret ingredient, but I can't say more."

Lillian smirked, and Naomi raised a finger to her. "And don't you tell. The recipe can't ever leave the women of this family."

The girl's grin turned to a giggle, and Naomi allowed a smile.

But she stole a look at Eric. Had she made him uncomfortable, unintentionally lumping him in with "this family?" He was, in a way, as Mary Ellen's father. He was connected to them. To Naomi anyway, and she to Dinah, who was married to Jericho. She certainly felt like she was part of the Coulter family.

And she would be in truth, once she married Jonah. Even her surname would proclaim it.

Her middle twisted, and she turned back to hand cups of chocolate to Lillian and Mary Ellen. "Be careful with this, sweetie. Careful not to spill."

She kept hold of her daughter's cup as Mary Ellen lifted it to her lips. She tried to pull the mug from her, of course, but Naomi maintained a solid grip.

They ate in mostly quiet, though Eric complimented the food, especially the sandwiches.

"Lillian made the bread yesterday." Naomi sent her a smile. "She's become an expert baker."

The girl's cheeks turned pink, and she dipped her chin, her smile spreading wide.

"If this is a sample, I'd say you could rival any chef at the finest Parisian bakery." Eric lifted his sandwich. "Well done."

That, of course, made Lillian's ears deepen from pink to red, but she managed a quiet "Thank you."

Naomi sent Eric a look of thanks. Lillian deserved to be acknowledged for her hard work. She learned so quickly and possessed an intuition that helped her hone her skills, both in the kitchen and in sewing. Her talent in those arts reminded Naomi a bit of how Dinah had been with doctoring. She'd spent hours each day with Pop in the clinic, and the times Naomi ambled in to see what they were doing, Dinah was always busy bandaging a wound or measuring out medicines. Pop said she had a special knack for healing.

"Want a bite?" Eric held out his spoon to Mary Ellen, a taste of pickled beet on the tip.

Should she tell him Mary Ellen usually spit that out? He'd learn for himself soon enough, though it might not earn him any favors with the child. Perhaps it was best their daughter didn't see Eric as completely perfect, the provider of only good things. That was an unreasonable view for anyone.

Mary Ellen eyed his offering, then glanced at Eric, and finally opened her mouth to accept the bite.

He obliged, but almost the moment their daughter's mouth closed on the spoon, her expression twisted into horror. She jerked away, then spat out the bite.

Naomi could only chuckle...until Mary Ellen stood and toddled away. "Come back. Mary Ellen, come back."

Lillian jumped to her feet with all the energy of a youth. "I'll get her." When she scooped her up, she looked at Naomi. "I see purple flowers on the vine by those trees. Can we go pick some to make necklaces?"

Naomi hesitated. Eric's entire purpose in coming was to spend time with his daughter. Yet he could hardly expect a child her age to sit still and converse with him. If he wanted to be with her, he'd have to go where she did.

So she nodded. "Stay where I can see you."

The two wandered away, Lillian telling the girl in happy tones what they were going to do.

Eric stayed across from Naomi on the blanket, munching the last half of his sandwich.

After a moment of quiet, he chuckled. "She certainly didn't like those pickled beets."

"I've never been able to get her to eat them. It's a shame because that's one of the few vegetables that grow well here. You can buy them easier in Missoula than most others."

He shook his head, his smile lingering. They ate a little longer without speaking. Should she say something about how well Mary Ellen was responding to Eric? He truly was a good father, making every effort—even at great cost. His long rides from Two Stones's village must be torturous with his broken ribs.

She didn't want to bring up their past, not yet. She wasn't ready for that discussion. The pain of it.

Better to keep their conversation on recent events. On their daughter and what a delight she was.

Before she could speak, Eric lifted his gaze to meet hers. "I just want to say how well you've done with Mary Ellen. She's a wonder. So precious. I know much of that comes from your hard work as a mother."

She started to tell him about all the help she'd had—she could never have done it without Dinah and the Coulters—but he raised a hand, and she stopped herself.

"I know you've probably been through far more than I'm aware of. I'd like to hear about it." His gaze shifted, a little wary. "Another time. But for now, I just want to thank you for raising our daughter to become the sweet princess she is."

His gaze held hers, his dark eyes so earnest, the compliment seeped all the way through her.

CHAPTER 10

"Thank you." A burn crept into Naomi's eyes at Eric's compliment. She held the tears back but let herself absorb the words that she'd wanted to hear for so long. She'd not realized how badly she needed this confirmation.

All those never-ending nights when Mary Ellen woke to nurse over and over and over. The times she was sick. The fear, the exhaustion. She'd done the very best she could, but it never felt enough. There was always the sense that she should have done more. Should have been better. Should have showered more love on the babe, not frustration. Not sadness.

The tears pressed harder, and if she didn't clear these thoughts, her barriers would collapse.

She forced a smile, and the action helped to lighten the weight on her.

Eric was watching closely. When she smiled, he let out a breath and looked toward where the girls were chattering among the trees.

Mary Ellen's sweet voice rose above Lillian's every so often, and Lillian answered as though she understood every sound the tot made. Lillian was so good with her. What a blessing to have her around.

"I've been thinking…" Eric's voice broke through her ponderings. "I'll need to go back to Washington in the spring when the river thaws. I'd like to take Mary Ellen with me."

Naomi's breath hitched, her mind reeling with the words. Hadn't he just said…? Did he mean a simple visit or…?

She inhaled a breath to quell the flash of anger. She had to make her words calm. Yet she couldn't keep from an incredulous tone. "Take her with you? For how long?"

Eric regarded her warily. He must be aware he'd dropped a burning ember into dry grass. "I want to get to know her. Let her meet my parents. Give her a safe life where she can play and grow up and…" The Adam's apple at his throat bobbed. "You could come too." He seemed to realize what he'd said, and quickly amended, "You and…your…" Again he swallowed. "Maybe you'd like to live in Wayneston again. You and…"

He stopped talking and lifted his gaze to the sky.

Was he hurt that she'd agreed to marry another man? She'd surely had the right to after he'd abandoned her without a single word.

But maybe he was remembering that night when he'd asked her to marry him. The words she'd said. That she knew without a doubt that he was the one God made for her. The other half that fit her perfectly. No one else could fill that place. God had made her for him alone, and him for her.

She shouldn't have said those things. They'd been true. But they gave him a power she couldn't let him wield now.

She took in a long, slow inhale, quiet enough he wouldn't hear. She had to answer him. And she had to keep their past out of this.

When she spoke, she managed to make her voice solid. "I can't believe you'd even suggest that. You'll have all winter to get to know her. She's open and trusting. She'll love you fully as her father in weeks, I've no doubt. But this is her home. I've raised her well so far—as you said yourself—and I'll continue to do so. You can come visit any time. Maybe when she's older, we can go east for a month. She can meet your parents and my grandparents."

A flash of sorrow touched his eyes when she mentioned her grandparents. Was he remembering how her own parents had cut her out of their lives. Nearly the same way he had.

Still, the reminder only strengthened her resolve. "Mary Ellen's home is here."

A giggle sounded from the trees, stealing Naomi's gaze for a heartbeat.

Lillian was tickling her, and the laughter that bubbled would make anyone smile, no matter how intense the moment.

It served to ease her anger a little. Though she disagreed with Eric, he would desire the best for their daughter.

She moved her focus back to Eric, softening her tone. "She's happy here, Eric. This is a good place for her. A wonderful place to grow up. Surely you want the best for her."

His eyes flashed, his shoulders squaring. He seemed to be choosing his answer carefully, and when he finally spoke, his voice sounded like a restrained mountain lion. "A good place for her? With—"

A scream split the air.

Naomi sprang to her feet and sprinted toward the girls. She could see Lillian's pale blue dress through the trees, but where was Mary Ellen?

Eric ran at her side, but when they reached the trees, he pushed ahead. These blasted skirts wouldn't let her move fast enough.

Don't let her be hurt.

When she reached Lillian, Eric had already scooped Mary Ellen up in his arms. Naomi gripped the older girl's shoulders as she struggled for breath. "What's wrong? What happened?"

Lillian trembled, but she lifted a hand to point ahead.

Naomi jerked her focus that direction.

Her heart climbed into her throat.

A black bear was fleeing on all fours through the woods, about twenty strides away..

She let out a shaky breath, pulling Lillian against her. "Thank the Lord."

Lillian clutched her as they both struggled to regain their composure. Naomi glanced at Eric, who was gripping their daughter tight, his expression a fierce mask as he glared in the direction the bear had gone.

"It won't hurt us." She still sounded winded. "It's just a black bear. They usually keep their distance."

"Usually?" The word was more demand than question.

"It's running, isn't it?"

He speared a look at her. "Will it come back?"

She shook her head, drawing in another full breath. "No. We're safe. All of us." She settled her focus on her daughter, who laid her head on Eric's shoulder, her thumb tucked in her mouth. She likely hadn't been afraid of the bear as much as the reactions of those she trusted.

Naomi moved to Eric's side and smoothed Mary Ellen's hair from her face. She made her voice bright. "It's all right, sweet one. Do you want to come drink more of your chocolate?"

The girl straightened, lifting her head from Eric's shoulder. "Cha."

Naomi lifted her daughter's hand to plant a kiss on her pudgy fingers. "Yummy chocolate."

She stepped back and glanced at Eric. She'd been close to him, but with the barrier of their daughter between them, she hadn't really felt the spark of his nearness. Mostly.

His jaw remained clenched and his gaze distant. Was he angry about the bear? Or about their conversation? She couldn't even remember the last thing they'd said.

She'd been trying to settle things between them. To help him see that they both wanted the best for their daughter. And surely they couldn't find a better life for Mary Ellen than growing up here in these majestic mountains, surrounded by her mother and a host of people who loved her. If only Eric could stay here in her life, too, though she wouldn't say that. He would have to be the one to choose that path if he wanted it.

She turned back to the clearing. "Let's finish our meal. The air is growing colder, so we should get back to the house soon."

Eric motioned her ahead of him. Perhaps he wanted to position himself between them and the long-disappeared bear. She didn't argue, just moved in behind Lillian as they walked single-file to the clearing.

When they reached the blanket, Lillian plopped down and picked up her cup of likely-cool chocolate. The flask she'd carried it in would have kept it warm, but these cups exposed the drink to cold air.

Naomi lowered to kneel where she'd sat before. Was it worth trying to finish eating, or should she start packing the food away?

Eric stood at the edge of the blanket, Mary Ellen still in his arms as he stared toward the woods. That hard set to his jaw meant he hadn't released his anger. Or perhaps it was more worry and fear for their safety.

No matter what fueled his tension, Naomi had a feeling this experience had only solidified his desire to take Mary Ellen back with him in the spring.

She wouldn't let that happen. She couldn't lose her daughter. And there was no way she would ever move back the east, not to the place where all the memories and reminders would torment her.

She'd found peace in these mountains, at least more than any other place. And she would do anything to keep this new life *and* her daughter. Anything.

CHAPTER 11

*E*ric glanced at the gray sky as his horse maneuvered up the slope to the ranch house. He should arrive in time for the family's church service. He'd been surprised at the invitation, surprised that they went to the trouble to have a service at all, though Dinah had said it would be a casual affair. Of course, living out here so far from any town or even a neighbor, they would have to hold their own services if there were to be any.

A tiny blur of white drifted in front of his face, landing with a sting on his nose. He glanced upward. *Snow? Really, God?*

The sky had been thick with low gray clouds all morning, so he'd known snow was possible. Yet, couldn't God have held it off until he spent a bit of time with his daughter and returned to the village?

Now he'd have to keep an eye on the snowfall while he was at the Coulters', and he might even have to leave early to make it back safely.

That single flake turned into a multitude by the time the house and barn came into sight. When he slipped out of the saddle in front of the barn door, his frozen feet almost didn't hold him up. He managed to make them work and settled his gelding in the stall Miles said he'd keep open for him, then pulled his collar back up around his neck for the walk up to the house. Everyone must already be there. With so many bodies inside, the place would be crowded.

Eric trudged through the rapidly thickening curtain of snow. The crunch underfoot was eerily loud in the silence as he approached the house. The icy wind cut through his layers of clothing, gnawing at his resolve as well as his skin.

He was about to face all the Coulters. In one place. Including Jonah. Would the man throw him out? The only time they'd been in close proximity since the fight had been the day of Sean's accident. Jonah usually kept his distance, so hopefully he'd do the same today.

When Eric reached the cabin door, he raised his hand to knock, but hesitated. Dinah had told him he could come on in without knocking. That they would be expecting him. Did he dare take her at her word? Naomi's sister had certainly accepted his presence there more readily than many of the others.

He moved his hand to the latch string and tugged. They'd left this hanging out, so maybe they really did mean for him to come in. As he pushed open the cabin door, warmth and the sound of voices blew out to greet him. He stepped onto the stoop and knocked the snow from his boots, then entered.

The warmth that enveloped him was so complete it almost took his breath away. He squinted as he adjusted to the dimly lit room, bustling with voices and movement, a stark contrast to the quiet outside.

A few women worked at the cookstove, and some of the men were pulling chairs into a large circle. The others clustered in groups, talking. He scanned their faces for Mary Ellen's cherubic smile. Or Naomi's.

They were already coming toward him, the mother carrying the child. A longing pressed in his chest. Naomi was so beautiful, especially when she looked at him with that light in her eyes. Now that she'd had time to think through what he'd said during her picnic, maybe she could see the sense in his words.

And their daughter... He could barely breathe with the weight of his wanting. If only he could go to them. Wrap his arms around them and hold them close. Never ever let either of them go.

When Naomi reached him, she didn't fully meet his gaze. "I'm surprised you came, what with the snow starting." She nodded toward a chair. "We're getting ready to begin. Sit there and I'll put Mary Ellen in your lap."

If only he could protest her constant coddling of his ribs. But she was right. Holding his daughter often made his middle burn so much that his lungs could barely draw breath.

He obeyed, and as she settled their daughter on his leg. The others moved to the chairs gathered in a large circle around the room. Lillian sat on one side of him, and Dinah on the other, with Jericho settling on her other side. Naomi sat a few chairs down beside Jonah, her gaze focused ahead.

Eric wouldn't have guessed there were enough seats for everyone, but somehow there were. Everyone except Sean, anyway, who sat on the floor in front of Jericho, legs extended in front of him. Perhaps Eric had taken his chair.

Before he could offer to switch with the boy, a hush fell over the group, and Jericho spoke up, his voice carrying through the room. "Let's start with prayer."

Eric bowed with the rest and tried to keep his mind focused on the words being said. Jericho's prayer sounded much like a conversation with God, mostly focused on thankfulness for the bounty of their lives, even in the face of challenges. His deep voice resonated with conviction. Clearly, the man's faith was a deep part of himself.

As the prayer concluded with a chorus of "amens," Jericho

looked to Lillian. "Want to start us off with 'O Worship the King?' You can pick the second one."

The girl grinned, a touch of pink tinging her cheeks. But then she opened her mouth in a lovely soprano. Her voice shook a little at first but gained strength as other voices joined in. This had been one of the hymns the church in Wayneston sang often, so Eric knew the words. When they entered the chorus, he couldn't help but glance at Naomi. Did she remember standing across the aisle from him, singing this very song? If he listened intently, he could pick out her smooth cadence among the others. That clear alto harmony.

He couldn't watch her long or he'd be noticed. Besides, Mary Ellen was squirming on his lap. He turned her so she was facing him, perched on his knees. He sang directly to her, which occupied her focus for a few lines as she studied him, brows drawn in focus.

When she grew bored and tried to get away, aiming for the floor, he turned her so he could clap her hands with the beat. That engaged her for almost a whole minute before she grew restless. By the end of the second song—"Joy to the World," which Lillian started with a confidence that made it clear this was a favorite—he'd exhausted all the ways he could think of to occupy his daughter.

He glanced at Naomi to see if she wanted to help. Not that he'd ask her to, but maybe she had a trick for keeping her silent during services.

Naomi met his look with a quiet smile, then turned forward again. Clearly he was on his own. But then Naomi glanced his way again, then pressed her palms together and laid them against her cheek.

Was it time for a nap? Yes, this might be about the time Mary Ellen had gone down the other days he'd been here. Should he take her to her to the crib? Surely Naomi would make that clear if she meant for him to. And he had a feeling that being stuck in her crib, knowing all these people were out here, would make Mary Ellen restless and fussy.

Instead, he lifted her to his shoulder, and she laid her head on him. This position put extra pressure on his ribs, but he leaned against the chair back to help support her.

The last hymn ended, and Jude rose and stood before them. He held a Bible and glanced at Eric as he began speaking. "We usually each take a Sunday to share a few verses of Scripture and how God's using them in us." He sent a quick look at the others before focusing on the page in his hands. "My passage today is from Jeremiah 55."

As Jude read the first half of the chapter, he focused on the verses that spoke of God's ways being higher than man's.

Eric had read that section before, but it always made him a little frustrated. If only God would give a hint about what He was planning, it would be easier to trust that He truly was leading. That the troubles Eric faced—especially since first leaving Naomi to help his father in the business—were really leading toward an end goal, not merely obstacles in place for Eric to find a way through.

After reading the scripture, Jude spoke of his journey back from New York City and how God had used the events to prove the truth in these verses. He laid out the details of how Angela had been assigned to follow him back to the ranch, how he'd hit his head and lost some of his memories. There'd been something about pretending they were married—Jude shared a smile with his intended that showed there were a lot more stories there. Jude used the story of what he and Angela had been through to show how God had used each piece as a thread in His master tapestry, bringing Angela to faith in Jesus and creating a love between them that was, if they way they looked at each other proved anything, clearly thriving.

Eric had liked Jude ever since meeting him in Fort Benton. The man was quiet, earnest, and appeared to possess a lot of wisdom. Angela seemed perfect for him—also quiet, as well as intelligent and kind. She fit in well with this group, too, so much so that it was hard to believe she'd arrived at the ranch the same day Eric had. They'd accepted her so quickly and easily, as if she'd always been part of this clan.

Longing wove through Eric, though he wouldn't linger on such a silly notion. He wasn't a Coulter, nor did he have any desire to live in this dangerous land, so far from his life and work back in Washington D.C. It was peaceful here, he'd grant, but there was no business. No industry. No shipping lines or means to transport massive amounts of goods. He'd spent the last two years expanding his father's export business, an accomplishment he was proud of.

When Jude finished his story, he bowed his head to lift a prayer heavenward.

Eric dipped his chin with everyone else, and the weight on his shoulder sifted into his awareness. Had his daughter fallen asleep? She'd stopped moving. In fact, she hadn't moved or made a sound in a while.

He laid his cheek against her soft, baby-fine curls. She smelled so good, like no other aroma he could recall. Did all babies have this scent, or was it unique to Mary Ellen? He let his body relax, trying to focus on Jude's prayer. But the sweetness of holding his sleeping daughter... She trusted him enough, felt comfortable enough with him, that she could doze in his arms. The weight of that faith wrapped around him like a warm hug.

He wanted to cling to the moment, to keep her safe and close, allowing nothing else to intrude. But the prayer ended, and a scattering of "amens" signaled a return to reality. The others began to rise, stretching and murmuring.

"Look at that snow." One of the younger Coulter men peered out the window behind the large table. "It's falling so thick, bet you can't see your hand in front of your face."

Apprehension tightened Eric's middle. He should have

checked the snowfall before now. Carefully, he adjusted his hold on Mary Ellen, then used one hand to push himself up from the chair. Familiar fire seared through his ribs, but he managed to keep his howl down to a grunt as he reached his feet. He paused a second to catch his breath, taking in tiny sips of air until the pain eased.

Then he moved closer to the window, standing behind the brothers clustered there. There wasn't much to see except a solid wall of white just beyond the glass.

A knot balled in his gut. This could be bad. He had to leave immediately or he might not make it back to the village.

He turned to look for Naomi, but she was right behind him.

Worry filled her eyes. "You can lay her in the crib." She turned and started for one of the back rooms, the one they'd taken Sean into the day of his injury.

Eric followed, slowing when he stepped into the dim chamber. Two narrow beds, along with a dresser, a couple of chairs and trunks, and a crib against the far wall. Naomi stood beside it, waiting for him. He crossed to her, then eased Mary Ellen off his shoulder and laid her down, his ribs burning as he bent. As long as he didn't breathe, he could keep from showing the pain.

Naomi arranged a small quilt over their daughter, tucking it gently around her, making sure she was snug and warm. She moved with such maternal grace, her touch soft and steady, a testament to the many times she must have performed this routine. Eric lingered by the crib, watching Mary Ellen's chest rise and fall in a rhythm that pulled at his heart with strings he hadn't even known existed.

He lifted his gaze to Naomi, who was gazing their daughter. The love in her eyes nearly made her glow. Exactly like the angel she was.

She must have felt his attention, for she glanced at him. Those beautiful brown eyes still held a vulnerable tenderness that made something ache deep within his chest. These two females...they were the most important people in his life. If only this moment of connection could last forever.

But then Naomi's gaze flicked toward the open door, and her brow furrowed. "I think the weather's turned awful." Her whisper was filled with worry.

The reminder felt like a plunge into the snow piling up outside. He didn't want to think about what lay ahead in the ride back to the village. "I'd better go."

"It's too dangerous. I'll talk to Jericho. Maybe you can stay here."

A new tension pulled in his chest. Stay? With all these Coulters? Jonah would probably rather see him freeze to death in a blizzard than lodge on the ranch, so close to Naomi and Mary Ellen.

He couldn't help a quick glance at his daughter. She slept so peacefully, completely unaware of the tempest swirling between those she loved. As it should be.

Naomi seemed to be waiting for his permission to ask. With all that worry clouding her eyes, how could he say no? And in truth, he had no desire to die in the snow today. He'd much rather stay in a warm cabin with his daughter and the woman he... Well, with his daughter's mother.

So he nodded. "If it won't cause trouble."

"Good." Naomi turned and swept quietly toward the door. He allowed a final look at their sleeping princess before following.

Most of the family had gathered near the fireplace, drawing chairs in closer to form several rows around the warmth. The howling of the wind outside could just be heard above the hum of voices.

Jonah stood by the window, his gaze focused on the pair at the door—Naomi and Jericho. Did Jonah guess what she was asking? What did he think about the situation? That glare must mean he surely didn't like it.

Eric moved his focus to Jericho, who was listening intently to Naomi, his expression hard to read. He answered her, though Eric couldn't hear his words, then pulled the latch.

A cold gust swept in, scattering powdered snow like spilled milk. The drift on the stoop rose up as high as Jericho's knees.

He slammed the door against the relentless wind, his face set as he brushed powder from his shirt. "No one is leaving." His voice held a finality that brooked no argument. "The storm's settled in. It could be hours, or it could be days."

He turned to Eric. "You can stay in the bunkhouse with the men. There's plenty of room there." It was an offer voiced like a command, one Eric wouldn't argue.

Jonah turned then, eyes locking with Eric's before he gave a curt nod. The message was clear...though the offer of shelter was begrudging, Jonah wouldn't turn him out into the storm.

Eric dipped his chin. "Thank you."

Before Jericho could respond, Sean's young voice rose above the rest. "Hey, Angela. Today's the kind of day you said for the chess... What'd you call it?"

All eyes turned to the dark-haired woman. Her cheeks tinged with color, but she smiled at the boy, a gleam entering her dark eyes. "A chess tournament. And you're exactly right." She addressed the rest of the group. "Who's in? If you don't already know how to play, now is the perfect time to learn."

It seemed everyone agreed to participate, even those who'd never played the game. At least they would have something to occupy them during the long day in the cabin.

No matter what, Eric wouldn't let himself be drawn into another fight, regardless of long he was forced to try to ignore Jonah Coulter's glares.

CHAPTER 12

*E*ric opened his eyes in the darkness but kept himself still as he took in his surroundings. The bunkhouse at the Coulter ranch. He lay on one of the top bunks, not close to the fireplace, but warm enough. He'd rather be here than outside, where the wind never ceased.

Was that what awakened him? He doubted it, considering the constant howl had lulled him to sleep, the unending whoosh and wail of the mountain gusts. A treacherous country, this land.

Another sound melded with the gusts, and he strained to hear. Was it simply a different wind, varying the pitch?

No. A baby.

His baby, crying. Mary Ellen. It had to be.

He raised up on an elbow and glanced toward the fire. The flames had died to a bare flicker among the glowing coals, which meant it must be a little after midnight. Did she still wake to eat at night? He would have thought she'd slept through the night for a while now. Hadn't Naomi said so? They'd talked about her schedule a little. Maybe he'd misunderstood.

The cry surged again. That was pain, not hunger. Something was wrong.

He eased down from the bunk, taking every precaution not to wake the others. Especially Jonah. The last thing he needed was the man barging in when it was Eric's right to help. *His* daughter was hurting. Not Jonah's. Not yet, anyway. And that man would never truly be her father.

Eric pulled on his boots and coat, then tiptoed to the door. He couldn't remember if the hinges squeaked. He'd need to slip out quickly, just in case someone awoke.

He accomplished the feat as far as he could tell, though the cold that seeped in might've pulled someone from slumber.

The wind... He tucked his chin in his collar and his hands into his coat pockets as he trudged through the snow. The stuff came up mid-thigh, so each step was more like a march. He still couldn't lift his feet above the top layer, which was turning hard with ice that cut into his thighs.

The way his face and hands burned, it seemed possible they'd be frostbitten by the time he reached the cabin.

The sound of wailing intensified with each step, making his insides clench. What had happened? Surely Naomi was trying to quiet her. Mary Ellen must be inconsolable.

When he opened the door, the cries turned deafening, coming from the direction of the cookstove. Had she been burned? His pulse hammered. He stepped inside, kicked snow off his boots, then shut the door and squinted to see better in the dim light.

A shadowed figure moved in the kitchen area, and he stepped that direction. His eyes finally adjusted until he could see Naomi, holding their daughter and bouncing her gently, attempting to soothe her while using one hand to do something at the counter.

He raised his voice just loud enough for her to hear—but

hopefully not loud enough to wake anyone else, though they surely couldn't sleep through this racket. "Naomi."

She jerked, turning toward him. She looked discombobulated, her hair pulling from its braid with little tendrils curling around her face.

Why hadn't anyone come to help her? He'd expected at least Dinah to be there. "What happened?" He moved closer and held out his hands. "Can I hold her?"

She handed over the babe, and he took the warm weight of their daughter, fumbling for a moment before he secured a better hold.

Mary Ellen reached back for her mother, but Eric pulled her close, turning away. "There, sweet princess. You're all right. Papa's got you." She sat like a stiff doll in his arms, opened her mouth, and let out another piercing, heart-wrenching wail.

He looked back at Naomi. "What's wrong?"

Naomi opened her own mouth and pointed to near the back. "New teeth are breaking through."

He cringed. *Breaking through.* Those words conjured a painful image of a tooth forcing its way through gum like a nail driven through wood. No wonder his baby howled.

All he could do was soothe her, then. He did the bouncing step Naomi had taught him as he meandered toward the fireplace. The dining chairs had been returned to their places, so the rug was clear enough that he could sit and play with Mary Ellen the way they often did. She didn't seem in the mood for play, but perhaps he could coax her.

He settled in a chair first, ignoring the fire in his chest, just in case he needed to stand right away. Her doll had been left in the rocking chair, so he snatched it and made his tone high-pitched in the toy's voice. "Mary Ellen, will you play with me?"

The girl's sob lost a little volume as she turned to see the source of the voice.

He scrambled for something else the doll could say. "I like

your pretty dress." He moved the figure close so she could pretend to stroke Mary Ellen's woolen nightgown.

Her cry quieted even more, turning to something more like a moan.

As he continued the silly talk, asking questions, then answering them, Mary Ellen curled into his neck, keeping one fist planted in her mouth.

The warmth of her little body against his felt so good. He'd helped. Somehow, he'd managed to distract her enough to stop the tears.

Naomi had been working, moving between the door and the cookstove. Now she approached them, holding out something. "Here, sweet one. Suck on this." It was a balled cloth. Did she just need something to gnaw on, to distract her from the throbbing?

Naomi glanced at him, as though she'd heard his thoughts. "I packed snow in it. Hopefully the cold will help numb the gums."

Ah, wise idea.

She coaxed Mary Ellen to take it, and once dhr raised the ball of fabric to her mouth, she seemed content for it to take the place of her fist.

Naomi eased out a long breath, then sank into the rocking chair beside him. She turned her head so she could look at them while still resting against the chair back. "I knew the molars were starting to bother her, but this is the worst she's ever been when she's teething." Weariness hollowed her eyes, or maybe that was just the shadows. Either way, she must be tired.

He nodded toward the bed chamber. "Go back to sleep. I'll stay up with her." Even as he spoke the words, he realized he didn't know how long Mary Ellen would be up, or if he should do something besides sit here with her. Should he try to put her back to sleep? Naomi would tell him what to do, surely.

The corners of her mouth lifted, but he couldn't tell if it was a true smile. "Hopefully a few minutes with that packed snow will help her feel better, then I can put her back to bed."

Maybe that would be better. The crib was in the room where Naomi slept, after all. If she went back to bed, then he'd have to go in there to lay their daughter down. That felt far too intimate.

A memory slipped in—the other time he'd seen Naomi lying under a blanket. He pushed that image back as far away as he could manage. But his breathing had already sped up, his insides heating.

He forced a slow, calm breath in. Then the same out. He couldn't meet her gaze. She might see his reaction and guess what he was thinking. Besides, the memories of their indiscretion were still too close to the edge.

He'd done wrong that night. So very wrong. No wonder Naomi had turned against him after he went to Washington to help his father. He'd long since begged for forgiveness from God. He'd put it behind him. That would have been harder to do if he'd known that his sin had created a daughter. But he was a different man now.

One who was doing his very best to be honorable. Honest. Upstanding.

And now...a good father.

Mary Ellen's breathing had turned even, and she no longer made the little sucking noise as she pulled cold liquid from the cloth. He couldn't tell for sure if she was asleep though.

He caught Naomi's attention and motioned to their daughter.

Her gaze softened, then she gave a small nod. She smiled as she whispered, "Well done."

Warmth spread through him, both from her words and from the rightness of it all. At last, he'd been here when they needed him. For both of them.

He stayed in that place a few more minutes, letting the

warmth of Mary Ellen's breath against his neck settle fully inside him. He couldn't sit here all night though. Or rather, he couldn't keep Naomi sitting here all night.

At last, he looked to her with raised brows and murmured, "Should I carry her to the crib?"

With a small nod, she stood.

He eased to the edge of the chair and tried to stand using only his leg muscles. He didn't quite succeed, but he was able to hold in his grunt. These ribs couldn't heal soon enough.

He stepped into the bed chamber and positioned his daughter in the crib. He knew the routine, adjusting the quilt just so. The snow had melted in the cloth, so he carried it out with him.

Naomi stood near the doorway, closer than he'd expected. She held out her hand. "I'll take that."

As he handed her the wet fabric, she didn't quite meet his eyes.

Tension hovered in the air. She must be just as aware of their aloneness as he was.

She moved toward the fire and hung the cloth on a nail protruding from the mantle. When she turned back to him, her manner seemed hesitant. Moonlight spilled through the window, casting a delicate glow across her features, accentuating the shadows under her eyes. Silence enveloped them, save for the soft crackle of the fire and the distant howl of the wind outside.

She still didn't look at him. "Thank you." Her voice came out quiet, almost wistful.

"Of course." The words were nothing. Nothing compared to what he wanted to say. Longing rose up inside him, longing he'd thought locked tightly away. Did she want what they'd had as much as he did? They could forget the past. The broken promises. They could put it all behind them.

Start fresh.

They were both far more seasoned now. Wiser. For his part, he'd seen enough of other women to know Naomi was the only one he could ever love.

"I wanted…" His voice came out rough, and he cleared his throat. "I want to be here for you. For both of you."

If he took a step forward, met her in front of that fire, would she let him touch her? He would be chaste this time. He wouldn't ruin this last hope by letting desire take over.

There must be something in her that wanted what once thrived between them. If her love had been anywhere near as strong as his, it couldn't be snuffed out. Not fully.

For a moment, neither of them spoke. Finally, she looked up at him, and the light in her eyes drew him. His feet moved forward before he gave them permission. He stepped around the rocking chair to meet her in front of the hearth, stopping within arm's reach.

But he didn't touch her.

His breathing had become harder, and he couldn't blame it on his ribs. Her eyes were so hard to read. Did she want to test what still lay between them?

Or did she really want Jonah Coulter? If that was her choice. If she loved and *wanted* to marry the man…

If she wasn't just settling…

Then Eric would step aside.

Now his lungs could barely lift with the weight on his chest. He had to know.

This was the point where he would either step in or back away. And Naomi had to make the choice.

His throat tightened. "Naomi." His voice came out weak, so he tried to add strength. "I loved you then. I still do. I always will. But if Jonah Coulter is your choice, I'll respect it. I won't get in your way or make things harder for you. Just… tell me now."

CHAPTER 13

$\mathcal{T}$ears pressed, and it took all of Naomi's strength to hold them back. Why had she wanted this? She'd spent months mourning Eric's absence, and here he was. Here and saying the words she'd dreamed. The words she'd prayed for, longed for, ached for in the deepest corners of her being.

Yet allowing Eric back in meant giving up all the stability she had in Jonah. The confidence that he wouldn't leave her. That he would always be by her side, providing a home and steady support. She would be safe with Jonah.

She had no confidence of that with Eric.

What should she say? How could she know Eric was sincere now when he'd failed so miserably before? He'd never explained why he ignored her all this time.

Maybe that was the place to start. If he was truly sorry for abandoning her, if he was willing to prove to her he was different, then she could begin to trust him.

She let out a breath and met his gaze. "I don't understand what happened. You said you would be gone for three or four weeks to help your father in his business, but you never came back. You sent all my letters back, unopened. Why?"

He frowned, his eyes not reflecting the shame she'd expected. This was more like...confusion. He tipped his head. "What letters? I don't... I never heard from you. Not one answer to every note I sent." Now embarrassment touched his expression, and he dipped his chin. "I don't blame you. What I did that night, it was...unthinkable. I should have... I shouldn't have..."

He looked up at her, his gaze as earnest and full of regret as she'd ever seen it. "I'm sorry, Naomi. I shouldn't have let things get out of hand. I made excuses. I told myself that, because we planned to marry, it would be all right. I was weak, and I didn't protect you the way I should have. It was an unforgivable act, but...if you can find it in your heart to forgive me..." His throat worked, and his brows tented as he waited for her response.

Heat flushed up her cheeks. She hadn't wanted to talk about that night. "We both were at fault, Eric. I begged God for forgiveness, and He helped me put it behind me. I hope you can do the same."

He exhaled a breath, his shoulders relaxing. "Thank you. That means—"

"But what did you mean about the notes? You said you never received anything from me? I sent over fifteen letters. Two the first week you left, then one a week after that. Every single one was returned unopened."

"What? No, that that doesn't make sense."

"Each came with a line scrawled on the outside, *Return to sender*. Are you saying..." The truth was beginning to break through. "Are you saying you didn't receive them? You didn't write that?"

It hadn't looked exactly like his hand, but close enough. She'd assumed he'd written them hastily, or maybe in a fit of anger.

That had hurt so much more.

He stepped closer. "I never received a single one. I can promise you that on oath." He breathed heavily, as if he were fighting a battle with an unknown foe. "I wrote to you Naomi.

Over and over. The first time I penned on the train to Washington." He took a step back, gazed away. When he faced her again, he looked a little sheepish. "As soon as I realized I would need to stay several months instead of a few weeks, I sent a telegram *and* mailed a letter ."

"I never receive any telegrams, either."

Confusion clouded his gaze. "I stopped counting how many letters I sent. There were two more telegrams though. When you wouldn't write me back, I thought maybe I could get your attention that way. You didn't reply. I hurried back to Wayneston as quick as I could, but you'd disappeared." He glanced around the cabin. "I guess you'd already come here."

Was that a trace of bitterness in his voice?

But then he turned back to her. He held her gaze intently, as if searching for the truth. "You're saying you didn't receive *any* of my letters? Or the wires?"

Dread churned in her middle. How could this have happened? Why hadn't she suspected it? She should have. After…after the terrible thing.

She should have know.

Fool. She'd been a fool.

She shook her head to clear the thought before the memory could destroy anything else.

Eric must have thought her movement was an answer to his question, for he let out a long breath, propping his hands at his waist. "I can't believe it. Is the Postal Service really so unreliable?" He sounded like he didn't expect an answer, but she had to give him one. She couldn't say everything, but at least she could enlighten him here.

She swallowed to bring moisture back to her parched throat. "I think it was Harvey."

His brow pinched. "My cousin? Why?"

She pressed her mouth shut. "He worked for Dyson's, which

houses both the mail and the telegraph in Wayneston. He would have had access to inbound and outbound mail and telegrams. He must have simply not delivered them." *Please believe me. Don't ask more questions.*

Eric's frown only deepened. "But why? He has no reason to."

She couldn't tell him the answer, so she looked away, letting the fire's flames capture her focus. The dance of orange and red could be mesmerizing. She didn't have to think, just let her mind be distracted by that sight.

Eric was quiet a long moment, and when he spoke again, the confusion had cleared from his voice. His tone was gentle, maybe even uncertain. "Maybe we'll never know what happened. I assumed you were ignoring me because of what I'd done to you. I tried to find you, Naomi. I truly did. After you left Wayneston, no one would tell me where you'd gone. I feared I'd lost you completely, that my mistake had pushed you away forever."

He started to reach out, like he wanted to take her hand. But then he stopped and dropped his arm back to his side. "You haven't answered my question. Do you love Coulter? Or is there any chance for us?"

He looked like he was holding his breath, bracing himself for her answer. The hope in his gaze made her chest ache.

If Eric really could be trusted... If he really did love her...

Could she trust it?

She couldn't bear to lose him again, not like before. Her heart...it wouldn't take a second shattering. She'd barely managed to put the pieces back together the first time.

How could she say no to this chance? This was *Eric*. The man she still loved with every part of her heart. They could be a family, the three of them, just like they'd planned.

Tears sprang to her eyes at the overwhelming emotion.

She'd need to tell Jonah. She hated to hurt him, but he

deserved a woman who was free to truly love him. *Lord, help him find that person.*

Eric looked nervous, and her insides were itching to tell him her choice. To see joy spread over his face.

She took a step toward him, close enough that she could rest a hand on his chest. She had to look up to meet his gaze, and the hesitant hope there made her smile. She lifted her other hand to join the first, letting herself soak in his warmth, the rapid beat of his heart. "I love you, too, Eric. I never stopped, even when I thought the pain of it might kill me." Her voice cracked, and she had to pause for a shuddering breath to still rush of tears. This was the time for joy, not sorrow.

Yet through those long awful months she carried Mary Ellen inside her, the pain of losing Eric had merged with the pain of what his cousin had done, so much it was hard to separate one from the other. She should tell Eric about Harvey. He needed to know. Needed to know how she'd been sullied. But maybe now wasn't the time. This reconnection was so new, so fragile. There would be a better chance later.

He gripped her arms, his touch solid. Secure. She wanted to close her eyes, to relish the feel of him. After so long.

But he pulled her close, his eyes intense. "I'm so sorry, Naomi. I know exactly what that pain was like, but the thought of you feeling it too... I'll do everything I can to clear those memories away, to replace them with good. Only good."

She was pudding in his arms, with those beautiful dark eyes, those soft lips speaking such love. Filling all the wounded holes inside her. Soothing the raw ache that hadn't gone away since the day he left.

He pulled her closer, wrapping his arm around her waist.

She kept her focus on his face, and when his gaze dropped to her mouth, a tingle swept through her. *Kiss me. Now. Please.*

And he did. As much she wanted that consuming, desperate kiss she remembered from before, he pressed only a soft, feather-light brush of his mouth to hers. A caress, then he started to pull away.

She couldn't stand it, her body crying out for so much more. She reached up and pulled his head down, rising on her toes to meet him.

This time he met her with the passion she craved. A deep joining of their lips, the strength she wanted so desperately. Yet there was still a guardedness beneath. And far, far too soon, he eased back. His breathing was as ragged as her own, and his hands moved to her upper arms, holding her there. She couldn't be sure if he wanted to keep her from stepping away or coming closer.

"I can't." He sucked in breaths, his focus every place except her face. "I can't let us go where we went before. I-I can't."

Realization swept through her like an icy waterfall, dumping shame like mud to ooze over her. Had she learned nothing? She'd been just as consumed now as that other night. Surely she would have come back to herself before she'd allowed things to go farther.

Eric's grip on her arms shifted, and he ducked to catch her gaze. "Naomi." His tone held an urgency, and she forced herself to look at him. To hear what he wanted to tell her.

Those eyes searched hers, seeking out every bit of her shame. Her regret. When he spoke, his voice was gentle. "Naomi Wyatt, I love you too much to let us repeat what happened last time. You ignite everything in me, but I give you my word, here and now, that I'll protect you with all that I have. You can know for certain that when I pull away, it's not because I don't love you, but because I do."

Her tears wouldn't be restrained. How had God given her this second chance? This second opportunity with the man who held her heart. The one God had made for her. She was even more certain of it than she'd been before. God meant for them to be together. Now that they were both stronger, more mature,

He'd brought them back together to build the life He created them for.

As though Eric could hear her thoughts, he pulled her close, wrapping her in his arms and cradling her in his strength. Her ear pressed against his chest and their heartbeats melded into one.

CHAPTER 14

$\mathcal{T}$he morning sun glared off the blanket of snow, nearly blinding Naomi where she stood with the others to see Eric off. The wind had died down, though the air was still cold enough to freeze water.

Eric had been determined to leave. He was probably right. She needed to tell Jonah about her decision, and he would likely take it better if Eric wasn't around. But her heart ached at the thought of her intended leaving again.

He would be back tomorrow, though, at least that was his plan. She'd made him promise not to take dangerous risks if the weather turned bad again.

He swung into the saddle, settled, and turned to them all. His gaze only lingered on her for a heartbeat, though that moment made her pulse lurch with the warmth in his eyes. Hopefully none of the others had been watching closely enough to notice.

He raised a hand in farewell. "Thank you again for your hospitality." His words clouded so thick, the white nearly concealed his face.

On her left, Dinah spoke first. "Be careful. If the ice is too thick down the mountain, turn around and come back. You're welcome here as long as you need to stay."

He gave her a nod, then turned his horse. "I won't keep you out in the cold."

The animal started down the slope, and within a few more seconds, they disappeared into the trees.

The others were already turning to head back into the house. Lillian had stayed inside with Mary Ellen who'd been fussy all morning, but sucking on the rag full of snow seemed to help.

Dinah wrapped her gloved hand around Naomi's arm and gave a little tug. "Let's get inside."

Naomi walked with her sister. Maybe it would be best to confide in Dinah first. Saying what she planned to tell Jonah might help her prepare. And even if Dinah didn't like the change, she would be supportive. That would help Naomi gain courage for the conversation with Jonah.

"Naomi, could I talk with you a minute?" Jonah's voice sounded from behind them.

Her heart sank. Had he seen something that made him suspicious? She wasn't ready to talk with him yet. Soon, but she needed to work up her courage first.

She summoned a smile and turned. "I need to show Dinah something. Can I come find you after that?"

"It'll only take a minute."

Dinah's frown said she caught the tension between them, but she patted Naomi's arm before turning to follow the others into the cabin. "I'll see if Mary Ellen is ready for a snack."

Naomi watched her sister another moment, then turned to Jonah. This time, she couldn't manage a smile, but she did her best not to show her worry.

When the door closed behind Dinah, quiet settled between them.

Jonah hesitated for a moment, then exhaled, his breath crystallizing in the frigid air. "Have you changed your mind about marrying me?"

The question, so straightforward and weighed with meaning, settled heavily on Naomi's shoulders. There was no turning back from this moment, no gentle way to unravel the threads of hope Jonah had woven around their future.

"Jonah." Her voice was a mere whisper, betraying her turmoil as she replied, "I-I feel like I need to give Eric another chance. He's Mary Ellen's father."

Jonah's face remained solemn, but a hint of anger simmered beneath his tightly held self-control. He held her gaze, his voice steady. "If that will make you happy, then it's all right."

"Jonah..." She struggled to find words that wouldn't sound placating. "You're such a good man. You deserve a woman who can love you without holding back. I won't get in the way of that for you."

A flicker of hurt darted across his features before he regained his composure with a subtle clench of his jaw.

"All right." His voice was even, but she could hear the rustle of fallen leaves in it—a sound that spoke of things that were once alive now being trampled upon. "If that's what you think is best. I want you to be happy, Naomi." The knot at his throat bobbed, and she caught a glimpse of the Jonah she'd come to know. "That's all I've ever wanted."

Tears surged to her eyes as he turned toward the barn.

"Tell Jericho I'm going to check the stock in the south pasture."

She didn't answer—couldn't, for the emotions rolling down her cheeks had also lodged a knot in her throat.

He strode with purposeful steps, then slipped inside the barn door. Gone.

And hurting. *Oh, God, why does this have to be so hard? Why does good have to be so painful?*

She swiped away the moisture on her cheeks. If she stayed

outside any longer, she'd have ice on her face. Better to search for a cheery expression until she could get a few moments alone. Maybe when Mary Ellen laid down for a nap.

She trudged toward the cabin. Even though someone else had already broken the snow here, walking uphill in the thick crystals took so much effort.

Things would be better soon. She had to believe that. Jonah would realize he didn't love her in the way a husband and wife should love a wife. He'd see this was the best choice for them all.

When she reached the door, she paused to straighten and catch her breath. She scanned the clearing around the house. With the exception of the track to the barn and bunkhouse, and another to the outhouse behind the cabin, the snow was still unbroken. Beautiful, clean, and white.

The trees wore lacy finery, and the sky above was a pale blue. Nearly cloudless, which meant no more snow for today, at least.

A thin stream of brown rose from the trees. Was that...smoke?

Her throat tightened. No one lived anywhere around, and that smoke came from the direction of Jonah's cabin. Had a stranger camped there during the storm? Surely not. There was no roof on the structure, so they'd have been exposed to the cold. No human could have survived without severe damage to their limbs.

And they must have seen the smoke from this cabin. Surely they would have come here for shelter.

She pulled open the door and scanned the room for Jericho. He was at the table, his back to her, talking to Mary Ellen as she ate.

"Jericho?"

He turned to her, a smile on his face. His grin slipped when he saw her expression. "What is it?" He'd already risen and moved toward her.

She motioned toward the distance. "I think that's smoke out there. Do you think someone's out in the cold?"

Jericho stood and pulled on his coat as he took the two steps from the cabin to the stoop, then to the ground. He studied where she pointed, his brows drawn together. "We'd best go see." Without shifting his attention, he called into the cabin. "Jude, Gil, grab your coats and snowshoes."

Dinah appeared in the doorway, leaning out to look where Jericho focused. "What is it?"

"Smoke." He finally shifted his gaze, meeting his wife's worried eyes. His voice gentled. "We'll go see what's happening."

Naomi never tired of the gentle way this strong man softened around her sister. He had a way of melting Dinah sometimes, too, but not in this moment. She straightened her shoulders. "I'm coming too. If there's a person out there, they likely need a doctor."

Naomi nearly smiled at the sigh that leaked out of Jericho. "All right."

Naomi followed him inside and joined her daughter at the table while her sister and the others prepared blankets, snowshoes, and a few medical supplies. This had surely turned into more than the scouting party Jericho had planned.

* * *

The sun had risen high over the mountains the next morning by the time Eric entered the clearing where the barn and ranch house stood. He was curled up against the cold, but at least it wasn't very windy today. How could he be numb and aching all over at the same time? Smoke curled from the chimney on both the bunkhouse and the cabin, and he nudged his gelding a little faster, his body craving that warmth.

When he eased to the ground, the barn door opened and

Miles stepped out. He reached for Eric's reins. "Get up to the house and I'll rub him down."

Gil stepped from the barn before Eric could answer. "I'll walk up with you. It's too cold out here for my bones."

"Old man." Miles sent the parting shot as he pulled the shivering gelding into the barn.

He fell into step beside Gil, following the rope had been tied from the house to the barn. He could vaguely remember one of the younger brothers talking about the need for it—something to guide them if they needed to reach the barn or bunkhouse during a blinding storm.

Eric was shivering too violently to speak as they trudged uphill. Yet his mind wasn't numb enough to keep from wondering whether Gil wanted him alone to question him. Had Naomi told them about what passed between the two of them the other night?

If Gil knew, she would have told Jonah first.

He'd wondered if there was anything he could do to make that conversation easier for... But speaking to Jonah himself, or even approaching the man with her, would likely only make the situation worse for Naomi.

Perhaps she hadn't needed his help.

Yet Gil's first words weren't what Eric expected. "You missed some excitement yesterday." His comment came out in a thick fog of white. "We found a dying campfire out at Jonah's cabin."

Eric shot him a look. Was he serious?

Gil scanned the trees beside the house. "Whoever it was had already left with their things, but we could see where blankets had been laid out. It looked like maybe they spent the night there."

Just the thought of it sent a fresh shiver. Someone had slept in that blizzard. How did they survive?

Gil glanced at him. "You didn't see signs of anyone on your way in, did ya?"

Eric shook his head. He'd not really been looking though. Mostly, he'd had his chin tucked in his collar, curled up tight to stay warm.

"Keep your eyes open."

The cabin door opened before Gil could pull the latch, and a rush of warmth spilled out. Naomi stood smiled at him. "Hurry. You must be frozen solid."

Eric stepped across the threshold, the heat of the cabin embracing him like a long-lost friend. His bones seemed to sigh in relief. As blessed as the warmth was, it was Naomi he'd longed for most. He stood there, his gaze lingering on her beautiful face. She wore a smile that warmed his insides as much as the fire did his outside.

The cabin was quieter than it had been the day before, with fewer bodies inside. Mostly the women, it seemed. Dinah worked over at the cookstove, and Angela and Lillian sat by the hearth. Angela peeled potatoes and Lillian mended a pair of well-worn trousers.

"Pa!" The squeal drew his attention toward the little figure toddling from one of the back rooms.

A fresh flood of warmth washed through him. He strode toward his daughter. "Hello, princess."

He scooped her up, ignoring the bite in his ribs. The pain didn't feel like searing fire anymore, just an insistent knife poke when he used those muscles. He spun her around, earning a giggle, a sound he would never tire of. She flashed tiny teeth. He cuddled her close, breathing in her sweet scent. It was moments like these that made every hardship worth enduring.

When she pushed away, he loosened his hold, and she looked at him with her mother's bright eyes. He kissed her forehead, then turned to meet the more mature version of those eyes.

Naomi wore a tender smile that made him want to do whatever it took to keep it there always.

"She's missed you." Naomi reached to brush back a red curl that was so long it draped in one of Mary Ellen's eyes.

Eric let a smile tug his mouth, but he kept his voice low for Naomi alone. "And I've missed you both."

A blush tinged her cheeks. She grinned and looked away.

"How about some warm tea?" Dinah approached with a mug in hand. "Let him sit by the fire, Naomi. He needs to warm himself."

As Eric took the cup from Dinah, she examined his hands. "Can you feel all your fingers and toes?" She eyed him, waiting for an answer. Apparently, it wasn't an offhand question. She was quite serious.

He offered a tight grin. "Every one of them." They all burned like he was holding them in the fire, but he'd live.

Besides, any amount of pain was worth it if it meant he got to spend these precious hours with his girls.

CHAPTER 15

*D*ays later, Naomi stood near the barn, clutched tightly to her daughter so they could keep each other warm. "Say goodbye. Goodbye, Papa."

Eric's grin filled her insides as he waved from atop his horse. "Goodbye, my girls. I'll be back tomorrow."

"Pa." Mary Ellen offered the sound, but it came out quietly, likely because she was getting too cold. Even with the sun finally warm enough to begin melting snow, it was too much for the baby.

And they were nearing nap time.

As Eric turned his horse and rode down the hill toward the trail through the trees, a bittersweet pang twisted Naomi's heart. Hopefully soon, he wouldn't have to ride to Two Stones's village every day. He would stay here with her and Mary Ellen.

Yet perhaps she shouldn't assume he planned to marry her. They were basically courting now, but they hadn't had any time when they could talk about the future. She would need to wait until he was ready to declare himself. In some ways, they had picked up where they'd left off before. But in other ways, they were starting from the beginning again.

Well, except that this time, they had a child together.

Would Eric want to build a cabin in one of the clearings on the ranch? Surely he would, especially if she told him that was what she wanted. She'd been so looking forward to having her home just a few minutes' walk from Dinah's. The clearing where Jonah was building had been the perfect spot.

Jonah wouldn't, perchance, consider...?

No, that was his own project. He'd taken such pride in every part of it, worked to cut each tree and notch each log. It was his home, and he would find the woman one day to share it with him.

Lillian rode through the barn door, pushing it wide so Sean could ride out behind her. Lillian waved the hill to Naomi. "We're leaving."

"Please be careful," Naomi called back. "You're going to the east pasture, right?" Jericho said he'd be watching for them after noon.

"Yes, ma'am." Lillian sent a final wave before pushing her horse to catch up with Sean's fast-walking mare.

Naomi could hear the girl telling her brother to slow down. That he was supposed to ride in the rear because he was the youngest and it wasn't safe up front. Sean, of course, argued the point. The tone sounded argumentative anyway. They were too far aware for her to hear the words.

Naomi smiled at Mary Ellen as she turned back to the cabin. "Maybe one day you'll have a little brother to boss around, sweet one."

The baby regarded her with sober eyes, then laid her head on her mother's shoulder.

Naomi snuggled her close as she walked. "I know. It's time for bed-a-bye, isn't it?"

Once inside, she moved through the usual naptime ritual. Changing her diaper, sitting in the rocking chair while she sang "All Through the Night," then carrying her to her crib. The babe snuggled on her side and reached for a corner of the quilt as Naomi adjusted it around her.

How wonderful it would be to have another baby, a brother for Mary Ellen. But this time, Naomi wouldn't be alone. Eric would be there for every part. Through the long nights, sharing the load. She could be the mother she wanted to be. Strong and patient and loving.

She smoothed Mary Ellen's curls away from her brow. "Good night, my love." Then she turned and slipped out to the main room, closing the door behind her.

She had just picked up the broom and began to sweep when a frantic call came from outside.

"Naomi! Hurry!"

Was that Lillian? Heart pounding, she rushed to the door and saw the girl astride her horse, face flushed with urgency. "What's wrong?"

"Sean saw smoke from a campfire," Lillian explained breathlessly. "He rode off to see who it was. He wouldn't stop when I told him we should go get Uncle Jericho. I came back for help. I knew I could get here a lot faster than to the east pasture."

As the girl stopped to breathe, Naomi's mind spun. She had to catch up to Sean before he reached the strangers who'd built the fire.

She hadn't warmed up enough to unbutton her coat yet, so she only had to grab her hat and gloves before stepping from the cabin.

"Stay here with Mary Ellen. I've just put her down for a nap. I'll take your horse to catch Sean."

Lillian jumped from her mount, and Naomi gathered the reins and swung up into the saddle. Her mind scrambled for any details she might need to ask before she left. "You followed the main trail? How far down were you when Sean turned off?"

"Not far." Lillian pointed toward the southwest, her voice

quivering. "He turned toward the creek, away from the pastures."

Naomi urged the horse into a trot, though she had to slow as they entered the trees. She didn't travel this path enough to remember where icy boulders lurked beneath the snow. Her breath puffed out in clouds, and the swish of the mare's hooves in snow made the otherwise quiet woods sound almost eerie.

How far ahead was Sean? Was he being careful? She didn't have to go far before she reached the tracks showing where Sean turned off.

Fear bubbled inside as she reined Lillian's mare to follow. What if Sean reached the source of the smoke before she caught up with him? It could be the campsite of someone dangerous. She had to move faster.

Did she dare shout for the boy? That could give away his presence to the stranger and put him in even more danger.

She pushed the horse faster, but it took all of her focus to guide the mare away from low tree branches and around suspicious lumps in the unbroken snow. She almost forgot to watch for Sean, so when she glanced up to see him among the trunks ahead, her heart skipped a beat.

He was standing beside his horse. The scent of woodsmoke had grown stronger. Had he found the campsite?

Naomi scanned the forest. Something dark rested on the ground beside him. Maybe supplies or gear? At least there was no movement. *God, let this campsite be empty like the other.*

She pushed the horse harder, and as she came closer, she had a clearer view. The fire seemed to have mostly died, though recently enough that smoke rose in a thick stream. Whoever had built it had left all their supplies here. The pile beside Sean was covered with a blanket, probably to keep everything dry.

He waved her closer. "Hurry."

When she reached him, she dismounted as quickly as her trembling legs would allow, then gripped her saddle for a second as she found her balance. "You shouldn't have ridden off by yourself. Whoever this belongs to could be dangerous."

With her words, the reality of their position rushed in. She'd not brought a rifle. Why hadn't she thought of that? The owner of these belongings could return any minute, angry at their presence, maybe assuming they intended to steal.

She stepped to his side and wrapped a protective arm around his shoulders, scanning the area around the camp. Still no movement out there.

"Look." Sean's voice beside her was insistent, and he pulled out of her hold and pointed at the blanket-covered supplies.

It took her eyes a moment to focus on the patterned material enough to see what he did.

Then her breath froze.

A face.

Or rather...a *person* lay under that blanket.

One side of the face showed a closed eye fanned by wrinkles in the tanned skin. A few long, gray hairs peeked out from the blanket. A woman.

Naomi pressed her hand to her mouth.

Had this poor being frozen to death that morning? It couldn't have happened more than a few hours ago, for embers still glowed in the fire .

"Is...is she dead?" Sean's young voice sounded worried, and Naomi wrapped her arm around him again. She needed to check.

Before she could, though, the stranger's eyelids flickered.

She was alive?

Naomi released Sean and crouched beside the figure. "Hello. Are you all right?" She spoke a bit louder than usual, hoping her words would stir the strangers.

The lashes on her eyelid wiggled. She reached out to touch the crepey cheek, but with her gloves on, she couldn't tell if her body was warm. She tugged it off and brushed her fingers over the woman's skin.

She couldn't be certain, but it felt like the body might still be warm. She needed to feel for a pulse. And if this poor person was still alive, Naomi needed to do everything she could to bring warmth back into her. Right away.

Every second mattered.

* * *

The ride back to the village felt so much shorter when the sun was warm. Eric lifted his face to soak in the heat—well, relative heat, anyway—as his horse meandered the familiar trail. Mary Ellen had been all smiles that morning, eager to play and be entertained, and he was more than happy to oblige.

He'd even managed a moment alone with Naomi at the end, when Sean and Lillian went to saddle their horses, and he'd grabbed at the chance for a kiss. Not long, but a wonderful taste and a reminder that he'd not always need to travel two hours each direction to see her. To soak in her beautiful smile. To wrap his arms around her. And savor more of her kisses.

So much he'd missed these long months. He still couldn't fathom how their letters and his telegrams could have all gone astray. The Postal Service wasn't known for complete reliability, but so many letters couldn't have been lost. And the wires. The telegraph had a much better reputation for accuracy than the mail.

Hadn't Naomi said his letters were returned unopened? That hadn't been the case with the ones he'd sent. Could the culprit be someone in their house in Washington? Had his father or mother disliked Naomi and interfered with their correspondence, or had one of the servants do so? They'd never shown signs of disregard. And his mother made no secret of the fact she'd like to see him happily settled. Besides, that wouldn't explain the telegrams he'd sent directly from the telegraph office.

Could Naomi be right about Harvey? What motivation could his cousin possibly have to interfere in their courtship?

A flicker of movement just off the trail caught his eyes.

A deer?

He focused on the spot. It had been larger than a squirrel or a bird.

But when the figure moved again, a human form emerged from the shifting light and shadows.

A person dashed among the trees with youthful agility.

Gil's words from a couple days ago slipped back in. Someone had camped on ranch property.

Did Eric just see the son of whoever had built the abandoned campfire they'd seen? This child couldn't be here by himself. He'd looked to be about Sean's age, maybe even a little smaller.

Eric opened his mouth to call out to him, to let him know there was no danger, but the lad took that moment to dart away, sprinting off through the snow and trees like deer running from a cougar.

Eric pushed his horse forward, but with the first step off the trail, the animal plunged into a snowdrift, the icy white rising to its neck and above the top of Eric's boots. The frozen crust on the snow must have melted with today's warmth. This would be slow going on horseback, and the boy had already disappeared up the wooded slope. Should Eric go back and alert one of the Coulter men?

Probably.

Seemed a better idea than trying to follow. Who knew where the boy might lead him, and Gil had asked him to keep his eyes out for the strangers.

Eric reined his gelding out of the drift and back toward the cabin at a trot. He'd seen a path that must lead to one of the pastures, for it was always packed hard from hoofprints, and there had been new tracks that morning.

It didn't take long to reach that turn-off, and he guided his horse that direction. Should he call out to alert them of his presence? Maybe so. The last thing he wanted was to be accused of lurking where he wasn't supposed to be.

He raised his voice. "Coulter!"

He was moving away from where the boy had run, so maybe the lad and his family wouldn't hear his shout and be scared off by the thought of the owners searching for them.

"What are you hollering for?" Jonah's annoyed voice emerged from the trees, not far ahead of him. "Something wrong at the house?"

Of all the Coulters he might have found, of course the first would be Jonah. Eric reined in as the man became visible through the trunks. "Not at the house. I saw a boy, farther down the trail. Gil said to watch for a stranger. I thought you all would like to know." He shouldn't feel like he had to defend himself to this man, but he did. And that churned frustration in his chest.

"You sure it wasn't Sean? He and Lillian are supposed to come help after you leave." Jonah spoke the words like a jab. Like Eric couldn't be trusted alone with Naomi and Mary Ellen.

Of course, it wasn't a matter of trust, it was propriety.

And his past mistakes didn't exactly recommend him.

He swatted that line of thought away before the heat reached his ears. "It wasn't Sean. It was a stranger. About Sean's age though. He ran away like he feared I'd chase him."

Jonah motioned for him to turn around. "Show me where you saw him. I'll check it out." He clearly seemed to be dismissing Eric.

Eric spun his horse and headed back toward the main trail. *He'd* been the one to see the lad. He'd like to know for sure he was safe. Just because this wasn't his ranch didn't mean he would ignore someone in trouble.

He held his tongue as they moved onto the main trail. At the place he'd spotted the newcomer, he turned off without speaking—avoiding the snowdrift this time.

"This is where you saw him?" Coulter moved up beside him.

Eric nodded forward. "He ran up that slope. I knew my horse couldn't go as fast as he could in the ice, so I turned back to alert you all." Maybe he should have asked to bring one of the other brothers with them. That might have been a less risky strategy than riding with Jonah alone.

He wouldn't let the other man prod his temper this time.

Jonah pushed ahead, not inviting Eric to follow, but also not sending him away.

Eric followed, of course.

He seemed to be more comfortable than Eric with traversing the tricky landscape, so Eric kept his horse to the exact path Jonah's took. They were mostly following the lads footprints, though Jonah sometimes took a different route when the mountainside grew steep or the underbrush too thick.

The boy must be as nimble as a field rabbit to maneuver some of the obstacles he had.

After a quarter of an hour, a sound grabbed Eric's attention. Voices?

He called ahead quietly. "Do you hear that?"

Jonah lifted his head and reined in sharply, and Eric did the same. That was a woman's voice.

Naomi?

Her melodic cadence was imprinted on his soul, leaving no doubt it was her.

Jonah slipped from his saddle, so Eric did the same. He led his horse behind Jonah, stepping high through the snow even though he had tracks to follow. He couldn't see much ahead except the hindquarters of Jonah's horse. Maybe he should have stayed in the saddle.

When the hill leveled off, they tied their mounts to a branch, scanning the snowy woods ahead. Eric could see no sign of a person.

"Any idea who Naomi is talking to?" Eric asked.

Jonah shot him a look—was that surprise? Had he not recognized her voice?

Jonah didn't say, just pulled his rifle from its scabbard. "None. I can't imagine what she's doing out here."

Eric's started toward voices. Jonah's long strides caught him up fast, and in the places they had to slip single-file, Jonah took the lead. He certainly seemed to know this terrain better than Eric, and he was better at breaking a new trail through the high snow. Was Jonah as soaked through as Eric? From the waist down, the snow had drenched his trousers and socks.

His worry for Naomi kept the cold from mattering.

The voices came clearer as he and Jonah closed the distance, and Sean's higher pitch joined Naomi's. Relief swept through Eric.

Had he been wrong? Had Sean been the child he'd seen?

Much as he'd be embarrassed to have raised a ruckus, he'd rather that than find anyone in danger.

Buy why had Naomi and Sean come out here? And where was Mary Ellen? Surely Naomi hadn't brought the baby out here to this treacherous, snowy mountainside?

The underbrush gave way to a small campsite, where Naomi and Sean stood over something covered with blankets. What had they found? "Naomi?"

She spun to face him. "Thank God you're here. Hurry. She needs help."

CHAPTER 16

She? Eric struggled to make sense of Naomi's words as he strode to her.

Naomi crouched by the blankets and began rubbing her hands over them.

Eric reached her side and realized what she was doing.

An old woman lay there, eyes closed, face gnarled and cheeks hollowed from cold or hunger or both.

Eric's breath hitched. She didn't look alive. Did Naomi think she could restore life to her by force of will?

"She's still breathing," Naomi said, "and she opened her eyes a minute ago." Her tone was determined. "We have to get her warm."

"Who is she?" Jonah moved around the campsite, poking at bundles of supplies. "Have you seen the boy?"

Naomi looked up at him, eyes wide, though she didn't stop rubbing the blanket over the woman's upper arms. "What boy? We found her just lying here."

Jonah frowned and straightened, staring into the trees in the direction they'd come. They did need to find the lad, but if this woman were to have any chance to survive, they had to move quickly.

Eric crouched beside Naomi and felt the wrinkled forehead. Sure enough, she was still warm enough that blood must be flowing, but her skin was cool. He touched his fingers to her neck, just to make sure there was a pulse. Yes, though weak. He was no doctor, and that was probably what she needed, along with a warm fire and shelter.

He glanced at Sean. "Do you know where Doc Dinah is?"

Jonah spoke up. "She's in the east pasture with Jericho."

Good. Eric held Sean's gaze. "Ride to her as fast as you can. Tell her to meet us at the house."

Sean glanced at his uncle, maybe for permission. Eric couldn't see the other man without turning, but he must have confirmed Eric's order, for Sean sprinted toward the two horses at the edge of the camp.

Eric shifted his focus to Naomi. "We need to get her to the house. Do you think she's injured?" If she had a broken bone, moving her would be much harder.

"I didn't think to check." Naomi reached for the blankets. "I hate to make her colder, but I suppose we need to know."

Was there any chance the woman was coherent enough to tell them? He rested a hand on the blankets where her shoulder should be. "Ma'am, can you hear us?"

They waited without speaking. For his part, he held his breath so he wouldn't miss a sound. Her eyelashes fluttered a little but didn't part.

He tried again. "We need to know if you're injured. Can you tell us if you're hurt?" Maybe he should make it easier on her. He scooted farther down where he could reach the length of her, then rested both hands on her blanket-covered arms. "Do you feel pain here?"

No answer, but her lashes twitched again. Was that a yes or

no? He glanced at Naomi, but she shook her head, her eyes showing her confusion.

He focused on their patient again and moved his hold down to her legs, though he kept his gaze on her face. "Does this hurt?"

There wasn't even a flicker of movement this time. She lay utterly still. Part of him wanted to check her pulse again, but he didn't have time to keep doing that. Maybe they should assume she wasn't injured and get her to the house. They would need to handle her with care.

"It's her arm."

Eric jerked his gaze up at the tiny voice, but he couldn't find its source.

A glance at Jonah showed he might see the person. It must be the boy Eric had seen earlier, though that voice sounded more like a girl's. A youngster, at any rate.

"What happened to her arm?" Jonah spoke quietly, a kindness in his voice that Eric had never heard from the man.

There was no answer. The child must be behind the trunk of a large tree just beyond the camp. Eric didn't dare move, lest he frighten him—or her.

Jonah must have worried the same, for he eased down to a crouched position, hopefully making himself less menacing.

At last, that small voice came from behind the tree. "She fell."

Eric glanced back at the woman. Had she broken an arm, or was there an open wound? He lifted the edge of the blanket—multi-colored woven thing that was thick, maybe made of wool. He had to lift several more layers of cloth to see her arm. She wore a coat, but the limb he saw wasn't in the sleeve. This must be the injured one.

Still, the fabric of a shirt or dress covered the skin.

He glanced toward the tree where the child hid. Part of a face peered around the side, watching him. "Did her arm bleed like a scrape? Or is the hurt inside, like the bone might be broken?"

The child hesitated, but finally said. "Inside."

Eric spoke low for Naomi and Jonah. "We have to get her to the house. Maybe we can wrap her upper body in a blanket to hold the arm tight to her."

He started to do that very thing. The thick top blanket was likely critical for keeping her warm. He hated to take any of the covers away from her. He wrap his own coat around her as well.

He wouldn't be able to lift and carry her with blasted ribs, but if Jonah could carry her to Eric on his horse and hand her up, he could hold on the way to the house.

As he unbuttoned his coat, he shared the plan with Naomi and Jonah. Thankfully, neither argued. Jonah turned and strode the way they'd come. "I'll get our horses."

Working with Naomi, they were able to lift the woman's upper body and wrap his coat around her. He thought about buttoning it, but it was so much bigger than her thin frame, even covered with blankets. So they simply wrapped the coat as tightly as they could around her.

While they worked, he glanced toward the tree where the child had stepped farther into view. He had to look twice to decide if it was a girl or boy. The youngster was covered in dirt, with straggly hair falling from a hood, but the features were refined enough that... Yeah, he was pretty sure it was a girl.

Poor thing.

Eric's chest ached. A young child here with an injured old woman, probably terrified and unable to help. Why hadn't she come to the cabin for aid?

As Naomi moved away and began packing the meager belongings to take with them, he stayed beside the older woman, his focus on the girl as gentled his voice. "My name is Eric. What's yours?"

Her answer came even more quietly than the others. "Anna."

He smiled. "That's a pretty name, Anna. I'm twenty-five years old. How old are you?"

She spoke more readily this time, maybe a bit more comfortable. "Seven."

"My, you're big for a seven year old." A bit of a falsehood, though he wasn't certain about the average size for a child that age. She was certainly smaller than eight-year-old Sean. He offered Anna another smile. "Is this your grandmother?"

She dipped her chin in a slight nod. "Gamma."

The sound of hooves tromping in snow grew louder, but before he went to help Jonah, Eric gave her one final encouraging smile. "We're going to do everything we can to help your Gamma feel better. Will you come with us to the warm house so you'll be there to talk to her when she wakes up?"

He found himself holding his breath and praying she'd agree. Helping her would be so much easier if she came willingly.

At last, she gave a wary nod.

"Good."

He pushed to his feet and moved to take his horse from Jonah. Naomi had finished packing the campsite and moved to take his place with the woman and girl. Once Eric had mounted, Jonah lifted the woman, still bundled tightly in the coat and blankets, and carefully placed her in Eric's waiting arms. Naomi had continued the conversation with Anna, and though Eric kept his primary focus on the fragile bundle in his arms, he caught most of what the two said. Somehow Naomi managed to convince Anna to ride with her.

Jonah helped the two mount Naomi's horse, then moved back to the campsite and scooped up the two satchels and a few pieces of clothing that remained of their belongings. Where had these two come from, and how had they ended up out here in the mountain wilderness? Hopefully soon he, Naomi, and the Coulters would get the story, but for now, they had to somehow help this frail elderly woman survive.

Naomi led the way, following the tracks she and Sean must have made coming to this place. Since Lillian wasn't with them, she must be at the cabin with Mary Ellen. Was it wise to leave a twelve-year-old in charge or their active little girl? Lillian certainly seemed capable but...

What was he thinking? Naomi had come to save a life, whether she'd known that when she left or not. Lillian would do her best with their daughter. Perhaps Mary Ellen had even settled down for a nap. She'd seemed sleepy when Eric left.

It seemed to take an hour to reach the house, though it might have been a quarter of that time. When they entered the clearing, Anna peered around Naomi to stare at the buildings. Had she seen them yet? If she and her grandmother were the ones who'd camped by Jonah's cabin, had they ventured this far?

Jericho, Gil, and Sean stepped from the barn and stood to meet them. Sean was talking as they neared, telling the story for his uncles. "I followed the smoke, an' Lil' went back to get Naomi so she could come help. It's a good thing we found 'em when we did, cause—"

Jericho settled a hand on his nephew's shoulder, thankfully stilling the boy's ramble before he said something that might make Anna worry even more than she likely already was.

Naomi didn't stop when she reached the men but spoke as she continued riding. " Is Dinah at the house?"

"She has things ready," Jericho said. "Lillian is with her."

Eric kept his horse following Naomi's. Jericho and Gil both eyed the bundle in Eric's arms, walking alongside the horses.

He offered what little explanation he could give. "This is Anna's grandmother." He nodded toward the girl ahead of him. "She might have a broken arm and is probably cold and hungry. She hasn't woken, though her eyelids move a little."

The furrow in Jericho's brow deepened. He glanced back at Jonah. "Where did you find them?"

"About two minutes down the main trail, then southwest a quarter hour at an angle toward the ah...strawberry patch."

They reached the cabin, and Naomi slipped to the ground.

Gil took the reins from her, and Naomi helped the girl from the horse.

Anna was nearly little enough that Naomi could have held her like a tot, but she placed her on the ground, though she kept an arm around the tiny shoulders.

"Can you hand her down to me?" Jericho stood beside Eric's gelding, reaching for the older woman.

"Be careful of her right arm." He eased the frail bundle into the man's arms.

As soon as Jericho had her secure, he strode toward the house. "Sean and Gil will take the horses. Come in and get warm."

Eric didn't need warmth, but he did want to be there to help with Anna and her grandmother.

Inside, Dinah was in the kitchen area, but she immediately moved toward a cot that had been placed by the hearth. How had they readied this in such short time? Flames leapt in the fireplace, sending a thick warmth through the room.

Dinah met Jericho before he lowered the woman to the bed. "Let's get these wet blankets off. Whose coat is this?"

Eric cleared his throat. "Um, mine. That right arm might be broken. We were trying to keep it close to her."

She sent him an approving look. "Good thinking."

Within less than a minute, they had all the icy material off the woman and tucked her under a half dozen layers of blankets, with a warm rock placed by her feet to heat them. Dinah barked orders in a calm, steady tone. She certainly didn't have to stop and think about what else might be needed. She must have done this routine more than once.

Everyone jumped to obey.

Eric was asked to carry a pot of water from the cookstove, then refill it from a large bucket on the counter, and he did so without complaint—or mention of his pained ribs.

He'd survive. He wanted that to be true of Anna and her Grandmother too.

The only people who didn't move were Naomi and little Anna, who sat on chairs at the foot of the bed, near the warmth of the fire. The girl watched every movement Dinah made with her grandmother, her expression stoic.

Naomi had a hand wrapped around her narrow back, but the child sat upright, hands in her lap, eyes fixed. As though every part of her world depended on what happened in these minutes.

And that was likely true.

A girl so young shouldn't have to bear such weight on those small shoulders. She should be snuggled in a blanket, drinking warm chocolate, and laughing at silly jokes.

They might not get her to laugh at the moment, but maybe he could help with the rest. Naomi needed to stay with her—the poor thing shouldn't be left to feel like she was alone, even for a minute.

Meanwhile, Lillian stood against the wall, watching Dinah examine the grandmother's arm. Eric decided to enlist her help with a little project.

CHAPTER 17

*E*ric caught Lillian's attention and motioned for her to meet him in the kitchen area. As he shared his plan, her eyes lit. "Yes!" She managed to keep her excitement to a loud whisper.

She pointed up the ladder to the loft. "There's a dressing robe on the bed up there that's the softest flannel. If you'll get that, I'll make the chocolate. And she might like the cinnamon cookies too."

The waif needed more than cookies, but this might be a good start to help her feel at ease among strangers.

The ladder to the loft reminded him of the one they'd had in the barn back in Scottsville. He and his best friend, Nathan, used to climb to the loft and swing out on a rope tied to a rafter. They'd land on the wall of a stall, then swing back to the loft.

Harvey hated when they did that, as he was two years younger and too scared to swing from so high up. The summer he finally gathered the courage to take the leap was the season everything changed.

Their ridiculous adventure up the mountain they'd been warned not to play on.

The rockslide.

Nathan pinned under the boulders.

The panic to free him. To go get someone big enough to move the rocks.

The way his best friend screamed in pain, over and over and over.

Eric squeezed his eyes shut against those screams and clung to the ladder, doing his best to slow his breathing.

He was a grown man now. Not a terrified boy running for help.

The loft was large and had several single-person beds placed along the length of it. Lillian's was easy to spot, for girls' clothes were scattered all around the floor near it. Not too different than his own room when he was a lad. He didn't let himself examine any garments closely, just grabbed the wad of red flannel draped across the mattress tick before he moved back to the ladder.

By the time he reached the ground floor, Lillian already had a mug of chocolate and a plate of cookies ready to deliver to Anna.

Naomi was watching them, a smile softening the corners of her mouth as he and Lillian approached.

She bent to speak quietly to Anna. "Look, I see Mister Eric and Lillian have a special treat for you."

The girl still wore her coat and boots. She allowed Naomi to help her remove the threadbare woolen garment and slip her arms into the warm flannel robe.

"Now," Naomi said, "you can drink warm chocolate and eat every one of those cookies." Lillian had placed three on the plate, enough for a grown man—far more than a child should be able to eat.

But who knew when this child had last eaten?

Anna's focus shifted from her grandmother to the fare before her, and she accepted the mug and a cookie with a hungry gaze. She downed half the mug in a few gulps, and swallowed half the cookie almost without chewing.

Naomi began to remove Anna's boots, speaking softly as she worked. "Lillian, bring her a pair of your wool stockings, would you, dear?" She looked to Eric. "Could you sit with her for a few minutes? I need to start a stew going. I'm sure Dinah will want the broth."

He eased into the chair Naomi had vacated, and though it felt foreign to pull a child he didn't know close, Anna sank against his side as if they'd been friends for years. She still munched a cookie—her last—and was peering into her empty cup. "Chocolate is my favorite drink." Her voice was low, barely audible compared to Dinah and the rest of the adults speaking over her grandmother just a few feet away. "It's been ages since I've had it though."

Eric gave her a little squeeze. She'd spoken without being prompted. Did he dare press for more? Maybe better to simply chat with her. Help her feel safe. " Chocolate is my favorite too. Miss Naomi makes the best, and she serves it often."

Anna licked the last of the cookie from her fingers—dirty fingers, but that mattered little just now—and then her gaze shifted back to her grandmother. A quiet tension settled over her again. He couldn't let her fall back into that worry, so he scrambled for something to say. "Did your Gamma make you warm chocolate?"

"Yes, sir." Her eyes were still locked on the figure lying on the cot. "She had Cook bring it when it snowed. She said it warms the heart."

So the grandmother had been wealthy enough to hire servants. Or at least a cook.

He gave Anna's arm another little squeeze, like a sideways hug. "Your Gamma sounds like a wise woman. Did you live with her?"

The glanced up at him, her gaze questioning. Or maybe

searching to see why would ask the question. He shouldn't have asked it. His goal was to make her feel safe, not interrogate. He couldn't lose sight of that.

He gave her a smile. "I remember going to visit my Grandma Jones in the summertime. She lived in a little town and had a house right on the main street. I could walk to the mercantile any time I wanted, but my mama only let me buy candy when I worked to earn the money. Mr. Zimmerman at the livery would pay me muck the stalls, and I learned the better job I did, the more he paid."

A smile tickled the corners of her mouth. "Did you buy a lot of candy?"

He gave a firm nod. "I did. So much my belly hurt." He clapped a free hand over his middle, and her lips curved more, though not yet a full smile. "After that, I started saving the money I earned. Most of it anyway. Sometimes I'd use a little to buy warm chocolate at the cafe."

At his wink, she final allowed a full grin, one that flashed a missing front tooth and bright blue eyes that reminded him of Mary Ellen's, though hers were brown. It was the pleasure that made them feel so similar.

Anna seemed to realize her reaction, and she dipped her chin in sudden shyness. But she snuggled in a little closer, like maybe she was letting down a barrier between them.

The weight of her trust pressed in his chest. They had to do everything possible to help her Gamma recover, for he wasn't sure he could stand watching her face the pain of losing the person who seemed most important to her.

* * *

*N*aomi stood by the cookstove, letting her gaze linger on the strong man who sat with the tiny waif of a girl tucked under his arm. Eric was reading Aesop's Fables to

Anna now, his voice changing pitch and speed as he spoke for each of the characters. She couldn't see the girl's face from this angle, but she could imagine her eyes wide as she soaked in the story of the tortoise and the hare.

This might be their life one day. Not with Anna, but with Mary Ellen tucked against her father's side. Naomi working quietly to make their house a home, preparing hearty meals and special treats that would bring smiles to those she loved. And having Eric here to enjoy it all with her. To help bear the load, to look at her with that loving gaze, to wrap his strong arms around her and make her feel like she never had to face anything alone again.

A fresh sting of tears rose. Happy tears maybe. At least in part.

She couldn't ignore the other scene playing out, mere steps from where Eric and Anna sat. The frail figure of Anna's grandmother lay shrouded in blankets that seemed to swallow her delicate frame whole.

Dinah worked tirelessly beside her, the lantern casting a soft flicker of light that caught the strands of her hair as she adjusted something on the woman's arm.

Jericho sat in a chair on the opposite side of the bed, like a silent sentinel, his presence offering support without words.

Dinah had found a good man in him. One whose strength wasn't just in his broad shoulders and calloused hands from working the ranch, but in his unwavering faith and support for her, and for the rest of the family.

She lifted her focus back to her sister, whose tight-lipped expression didn't bode well. Dinah had a remarkable ability to mend wounds and spirits, but Naomi had seen that expression more than once. She must be worried they might lose their patient. Dinah would think of the woman as her patient, the loss as her responsibility. Naomi had to remind her of the greater Healer who was really in control of this grandmother's life.

She gave the stew a final stir. It needed to simmer a half hour before she served it. That would give her time to help Dinah where she could. She approached the bed, keeping her footsteps as soft as she could on the creaking floorboards.

Jericho stood as she approached. "I need to bring in more wood." He gave Naomi a significant look, one that said he would only leave if she would stay to help her sister.

She gave a nod, and he headed to the door. She moved to stand beside Dinah, studying what her sister was doing.

Dinah's hands moved quickly as she tied a sling around the thin arm and shoulder. "Her shoulder was dislocated, but I put it back in place. I'm securing it to alleviate pain and allow the tendons to heal." Her fingers fumbled with the knot. When working with a patient, Dinah was usually so focused, her actions rarely erred.

Naomi glanced at her sister's face as Dinah spoke again. "The pain from the dislocation might have sent her into toxic shock. That, combined with the cold, dehydration, and hunger... It's so much for her body to recover from, especially at her age." A small tremble crept into her voice. Was she saying the woman likely wouldn't make it?

Naomi slipped an arm around her sister, moving close so Dinah could feel her support. Dinah usually kept a professional demeanor, yet a tender heart like hers could only take so much.

Dinah took in a shuddering breath as she pulled the blankets over her patient's arm, tucking them up around her chin. Then she turned in to Naomi, wrapping her arms around her in a hug they hadn't shared in so very long.

Naomi held her tightly, breathing in her twin's pain as her own tears leaked from her eyes. Caring was so hard. It opened the heart to be vulnerable. To feel so much pain even about a person unknown—a woman who'd not even opened her eyes and spoken to them. But her loss would affect them. Dinah would need to heal from it.

Dinah clung to Naomi, her shoulders rising and falling with each deep breath.

Naomi sent up a silent plea. *Help her know how much she's loved. Show her that if this patient dies, it won't be because of anything she did or didn't do. Help her rely on You for her strength.*

At last, Dinah let out a long, slow breath, then eased back. She managed a tremulous smile, though her eyes didn't reflect it.

Naomi kept a grip on her sister's elbows, drawing her gaze. When Dinah final met her eyes, Naomi put every ounce of love and certainty she could muster into her voice. "I'm thankful God brought Anna and her grandmother so we can help them. But you have to remember this woman's life is in God's hands. There's nothing you can do to change that."

Dinah's gaze wavered, her eyes shimmering pools that threatened to overflow. She gave a short nod, the lines of her face softening with the acknowledgment of this inescapable truth they both knew. "Thank you, Naomi." Her voice carrying a quiver, but also the underlying strength that made her sister such a wonder.

Naomi released Dinah's elbows, and her sister composed herself, wiping her eyes. She turned back to her patient and brushed the back of her hand down the woman's cheek. Probably feeling her temperature, but also sharing the kindness that flowed from Dinah's very heart.

As Dinah packed away her supplies, Naomi studied the woman's small, wrinkled face. How many burdens had she born in her many years? Children who tested her, worried her, even angered her. Yet all those emotions came from the depth of a mother's love. And a grandmother's.

She slid a look back at Anna. She'd snuggled in so close to Eric that her head lay against his chest, one hand visible over the top of the blanket. That hand rested directly over his heart, maybe feeling its steady beat. The poor child must have had so much uncertainty in her short life. At least these last few days or weeks. Where were her parents? How had she and her grandmother come to be in such an awful predicament, wandering the mountain wilderness in a snowstorm?

Her heart ached at the thought of what they'd both endured —Anna must have been afraid they'd freeze to death, worried about her grandmother, hungry, and so very cold.

And the grandmother... She refocused on the older woman. How awful to know you were putting such a sweet young child, your granddaughter who you loved with all your heart, through an ordeal so awful. Yet she must not have been able to find shelter. Must have been doing the very best she could for her granddaughter.

Once again, Naomi's eyes burned.

Inside this still body, the woman surely wanted desperately to know her granddaughter was safe and cared for. And wouldn't be turned out, even after her guardian left this life.

Naomi eased down on the edge of the mattress tick. How should she begin?

She reached up to brush a lock of silvery hair from her forehead.

Naomi leaned close enough that the woman should be able to hear her, even if she was hard of hearing. "Ma'am. I'm Naomi Wyatt. Your granddaughter, Anna, is safe here with us." What details would be helpful? "We're in a warm cabin, the cabin that belongs to my sister, Dinah, and her husband, Jericho. Dinah is a doctor, and she's doing everything she can to help you feel better."

Naomi glanced at Eric and the girl. "Anna just finished drinking warm chocolate and eating cookies, and I have a stew simmering so she can eat a hearty meal. She's a lovely girl, and you should be proud." Naomi's voice quivered. How much had this woman endured to help Anna become the sweet, diligent child she was?

She did her best to keep her voice steady as she continued. "Jesus loves children, and He holds them close in His arms. He's watching over Anna, protecting her. And He's caring for you too. No matter what happens, you can trust that the Lord loves your precious granddaughter. He has a special plan for her." Tears leaked past her own defenses, flowing down her cheeks. She had one more thing to say though.

"I give you my word. I'll do everything in my power to make sure Anna is safe and healthy and happy, as long as I'm needed. Until someone from her family can take over, I'll care for her as if she were my own."

Naomi's blurry vision wouldn't let her see if the woman responded, but her heart said every word she spoke was truth and needed to be said aloud. She placed her hand over the rise in the blanket that was probably the uninjured arm.

"Please don't worry about your granddaughter. Or yourself." Naomi took in a breath and let it out. "Both of you—all of us—are in God's hands. Rest in that knowledge."

A hand touched her back, then rubbed in that gentle motion that had always been Dinah's. Naomi let herself soak in the support. The solace. The shared strength.

No matter what happened in these next few hours, no matter how each life here was changed, they would work through the trials and relish the joys together.

CHAPTER 18

*N*aomi pulled the door to the bed chamber closed as soundlessly as she could. As exhausted as she must be, Anna had struggled to fall asleep. Naomi had put the girl in her own bed since the other spare bed was still in the main room.

Her grandmother had passed in early evening.

The girl seemed to understand what happened, and a few tears had slipped down her cheeks as Naomi explained, but not as many as she'd expected. Perhaps Anna didn't fully understand, or perhaps she'd prepared herself for this possibility for days now. And maybe this sweet young child had experienced other deaths before this one. Her parents? Perhaps she'd guarded her heart to protect it from the pain of loss.

That thought made tears burn Naomi's own eyes once more. No matter what, she wanted Anna to experience the fullness of love. As long as she lived here, she would know unconditional kindness, compassion, and love.

But how long would that be? That was what they were all about to discuss.

She settled into the rocking chair by the fire, the one seat left empty for her. The rest of the family had already gathered and were waiting for her to join them.

Dinah sat beside her, and when Naomi had settled into the rocker, Dinah reached over to squeeze her hand. Naomi sent a small smile as she squeezed back. They were all in this together.

She glanced around at the rest of the group. All six Coulter brothers were here, along with Dinah, Angela, and herself. Lillian sat next to Angela, just like one of the grown women. She'd taken up a pair of trousers she was mending, as Naomi often did when sitting with the others in the evening.

Sean sat on the floor beside Miles's chair, both whittling with small knives. Miles had begun teaching the boy since the trip to Fort Benton, and Sean latched on to the instruction with a hunger.

This strong, caring family would make sure Anna had the best chance possible for a good life. If only Eric could have been here too. But he should be almost back to the village by now.

On Dinah's other side, Jericho cleared his throat, the sign he was ready to start the conversation. He looked to her. "Anna was able to sleep then?"

Naomi nodded. She'd expected him to start with practical matters, not the little girl's emotional state. "It took a little for her to settle. I think she's exhausted."

"No doubt." Jericho shifted his gaze to the fire. "I suppose we should wait until the sun reaches its strongest before we attempt to dig a grave."

She spoke quickly before her mind let her hesitate. "Can we wait until Eric comes? I'm sure he'll want to help. And to be here for the burial." He should be here now, for this conversation. He'd spent the most time with Anna, not leaving until nearly dark. She'd almost asked if he wanted to stay the night, but neither Jericho nor Dinah had made the offer, so she'd hesitated in doing so herself.

She should have though. He should be part of these decisions.

Jericho nodded. "We'll have to wait for the sun anyway." He glanced around at his brothers. "We'll bury her in the graveyard, near Mum and Dat and Lucy?"

The others nodded their consent, none voicing concern.

Jericho stared at his fingertips pressed together. "I don't suppose we should wait to bury her until we find more family." He looked at Naomi again. "What has Anna said about herself?"

"Her surname is Jasper. I don't know if that's also her grandmother's name or not. She didn't know her grandmother's Christian name. She was simply Gamma to her."

So little to go on. But a young girl would hardly be expected to know more. "She hasn't spoken of her parents, and I haven't wanted to ask in case that adds to her pain." She glanced at Dinah to check her sister's reaction. "I suppose I can ask her tomorrow."

Dinah's eyes glimmered with sadness, but no censure for her reticence.

Naomi looked back to Jericho. "The only other thing she's said that might be helpful is what she told Eric. She and her grandmother were traveling to a town where her Aunt Patsy had gone. Her aunt had married a man there. Perhaps they lost the road when the storm struck? That's the only sense I can make of why they were wandering around these mountains."

Jonah's voice joined the conversation. "Sounds like we should head to Missoula Mills, since that's likely the town they were headed toward. We can ask around for news of a Patsy Jasper, or perhaps just Patsy if she's married now." His gaze narrowed on the low flames licking at the logs in the hearth. "We've no way of knowing if Jasper is Anna's father's name or her maternal family name, which would make it Patsy's as well. Unless Patsy had been wed before..." His voice trailed off as he sank into thought.

"Sounds like the best plan." Jericho looked around, maybe weighing who should go. "Maybe—"

"I'll go." Jonah said. "I can leave morning after next. If I go alone, I can move faster. Shouldn't be gone more than three days unless I get a lead." His jaw held a stubborn set that said he'd made up his mind.

Was he so determined for Anna's sake alone? Likely he also wanted to get away from the ranch. Maybe even away from Naomi. Her chest ached for him.

Perhaps allowing Jonah time away would help them all.

"You sure you want to tackle that on your own?" Though Jericho's voice held steady, it also possessed an edge of concern. "You never know when the weather might turn. Having someone with you in town to help ask around would make the search go faster."

Jonah gave a slight shake of his head. "I'll get it done. You'll need everyone else here to help with the stock. Especially if it snows again."

Even she knew they could spare a man to go with Jonah, but Jericho must have decided letting him go alone was the wisest move. He nodded. "Might be good to wire some of the other towns in both directions to see if anyone has heard of her."

Jonah nodded. "Good idea."

Silence filled the space, bringing tension she wished to avoid. "I'll ask Anna more questions tomorrow. Maybe I can get her talking and she'll say something that's helpful." Surely the girl knew more than she had told them so far. Though she was young, she'd proven to be a smart, capable child.

"We'll pray for the Lord's guidance through all of this." Dinah's words drew Naomi's gaze to her sister.

The Lord's guidance? Yes. But what if He brought Anna's aunt to them and she was a horrible woman? What if her new husband was course and heavy-handed. Could she stand to release the girl to her kin, even if they didn't seem like they would give her a good, loving home?

Naomi's heart ached with the weight of the decisions they might have to make. She shouldn't let herself dwell on those possibilities yet. But the dread of them was impossible to push away.

* * *

*E*ric hoisted Mary Ellen up onto his lap at the large dining table with the rest of the Coulters. All except Jonah, that was. After five days away, he'd returned from Missoula Mills sometime in the night, but after telling Jericho he'd not found Anna's aunt, he'd gone to bed, promising to share the rest of the details this morning.

Morning had come, but apparently Jonah was still snoring in the bunkhouse, last Eric had seen him.

It was a relief that Eric had finally been invited to stay the night there too. He'd wanted to spend every moment here helping, so those first two days after they found Anna, he'd traveled the long journey to and from the village in the dark—late in the evenings and early in the mornings. In the afternoon of the second day, Jericho had pulled him aside and said it made a great deal more sense for him to stay in the bunkhouse, at least for now.

Did that mean until Jonah returned? He could understand Jericho not wanting another round of fisticuffs between them, but Eric wouldn't let that happen again, no matter where he slept. And though they weren't friends, they'd managed to get along for weeks now.

Eric would do whatever the eldest Coulter asked, but he was more than grateful for these last two nights when he'd only had to walk down the hill to his bed, not ride two hours in the dark, wrapped up against the icy wind that never seemed to stop in these mountains.

Naomi and Dinah were the last to settle into their seats, both sisters carrying plates piled high with biscuits that they placed in the center of the table. After perching in her chair, Naomi wrapped an arm around Anna beside her, giving the girl a side hug and a kiss on the head. Naomi had lavished affection on the child every chance she could, which coaxed a smile every time— though sometimes only a slight one.

Eric loved Naomi's heart and the easy way she drew in those who needed her care and love. But Anna would likely be leaving them, going to her family as soon as they located them. He wasn't sure he could stand watching Naomi mourn her loss. *God, how do I protect her now?* Anna needed this affection and love too. It didn't seem wrong to stop its flow. Yet, the pain of losing Anna would be cruel for them both.

"Shall we pray?" Jericho spoke the words that had begun every meal Eric had taken with these people.

But before he could bow is head, the cabin door flew open.

Jonah stepped in and trudged toward his place at the table. He looked rough, hair disheveled and his eyes rimmed red. Only from lack of sleep?

He plopped down in his chair, staring at the plate before him. "Why didn't anyone wake me?"

Jericho gave a steady response. "Thought it best you catch up on your rest."

A snort was Jonah's only reply, and he looked around at the others' empty plates. "You blessed the food?"

"We were about to." Jericho nodded to Sampson. "Will you, Sam?"

Eric bowed with the others as the younger brother spoke a quick earnest prayer. With the "amen," the tension around the table seemed to double.

Jonah must not have felt it, for he didn't hesitate, just reached toward the biscuit tray in front of him and grabbed two, plopping them on his plate. At the same time, he used his other hand to scoop a spoonful of beans and pour them out next to the biscuits.

The others served themselves, too, so Eric reached for another bowl of beans and ladled a small portion for Mary Ellen. Naomi had said to mash them so she had no problem chewing them. Were her teeth still hurting? He should have asked.

Jonah broke the quiet once more, his voice a little jarring, maybe because Eric had been deep in thought.

The man didn't seem himself. Coarser maybe. Not as mannerly as usual. "First morning in Missoula, I sent wires to the telegraph agents of all the towns along the Mullan Road, asking them to check with the town law and in the mercantile or dry goods stores to see if anyone knew of a—" He cut of his words with a glance toward Anna. The girl was eating quietly, not looking up at anyone. But it would be better if they didn't name her aunt. That might make her worry. Good thing Jonah must have realized that too. "Anyway, after I sent the telegrams, I asked at every single business in town, the ones that were open anyway. No one knew anything about who I was lookin' for."

He scooped beans onto his biscuit and took a man-sized bite. Apparently, he hadn't eaten much on the journey.

Eric spooned another bite of beans into his daughter's mouth, and she nodded her head as she chewed, making a funny face at him.

He wrinkled his nose at her, and she grinned.

Jonah swallowed his bite. "Started getting wires back that afternoon. I figured I'd better stay a second day to make sure I read 'em all." He took a swig of coffee and gulped it down. "Two towns I heard from said there was a woman...by the name we're looking for who stayed there a little while. One said a week, the other said two months." He tipped his head sideways. "Both of 'em said she was there for the Independence Day celebration, so I'm thinkin' they're not talkin' about the same person."

He took another drink and gulped it down, then plopped the cup on the table.

He'd definitely lost a few manners along the trail. He let out a long, loud breath. "Virginia City...well, they couldn't answer definitively. The law there said there may have been ten of the name there in the last six months. He couldn't say and had more important work to do. None of the store owners answered, 'cept one who said he didn't do a census of the women who traveled through town."

They had nothing to go on then. A heaviness sank over them all. Everyone except the mite in his lap anyway. She patted his hand, asking for more beans. He obliged, lifting another bite of mashed food to her mouth.

The "um, num" sound she made as she chewed seemed to cut through a layer of tension, for when he looked up, most of the others were watching her, a few smiles lightening their expressions.

They slipped back into eating, and the quiet lingered.

Eric took his own bite of beans as he worked through the conundrum of how to locate Anna's aunt. He'd seen maps of the Montana Territory, and the place looked expansive even on paper. And traveling through the landscape had made him realize this country was far more vast than any map could display.

If he'd not found the Coulters in Fort Benton, he wasn't certain he'd ever have found this ranch. That meeting must have been God-orchestrated, for how likely was it that he'd arrive at the very time they'd come to town?

We'd appreciate if You'd coordinate another meeting, please, this one with Anna's aunt.

If she'd come on the Mullan Road, as Anna's answers had indicated, she would have most likely come through Fort

Benton. That town was pretty much the gateway to the territory.

He swallowed his bite, then glanced at Jonah and Jericho. "Since there's not an obvious answer close by, perhaps it would help to go about the search methodically." All eyes turned his way, so he pushed on. "Maybe start at Fort Benton, since that's where most folks arrive in Montana. Can we check passenger records for ships that have docked there in the last two years?"

The men seemed to consider his suggestion, exchanging glances before Jericho finally spoke up. "Maybe." His expression turned thoughtful. "The ticket office might keep a copy."

He was quiet again, as his gaze wandered around the table, lingering on each of his brothers, and then his wife. All must have agreed to the plan in their silent communication, for Jericho finally turned to Jonah. "Weren't you hoping the rest of your glass shipment would arrive on one of the last steamers to come up before the river froze? Since you took on Missoula, would you want to tackle Fort Benton? You could handle both errands on the same trip."

Eric could only see the side of Jonah's face but didn't miss how his jaw tightened, and there was hesitation before he responded. "I guess that makes sense."

If he didn't want to handle it, perhaps it was better he didn't. Inspecting the passenger records meticulously would require both patience and an eye for detail—the kind of scrupulous attention that might mean spending days poring over lists and ledgers. The name Patsy could be short for Patricia, Patty, or countless other names. They had to be thorough.

The more Eric thought, the more certainty pulsed through his veins. He needed to be there for that part. Thorough attention to detail was part of his role in LaGrange Exports, and one of the skills that helped him excel in his dealings.

"I'd like to go along and help with the search."

Once more, the attention of all homed on Eric. Jonah's eyes

had narrowed, though he didn't look angry. Maybe just deep in thought.

Something in the way Naomi moved drew his gaze toward her. Her face had paled. Was she worried about him and Jonah traveling together? That was a valid concern, one he should address.

He shifted his focus between Naomi and Jericho as he spoke. "I'm good at digging through records. I'll do my best to help on the journey, or at least stay out of the way." He let his lips tug up in a grin and tried for a lighter tone. "And when we get to Fort Benton, I don't mind sitting in front of a ledger for days on end."

Naomi's mouth curved a little, but the worry lines didn't leave her brow.

Jericho let out a sigh. "I suppose it will go faster with two handling the search." He turned to face his brother. "You all right with that?"

Jonah gave a curt nod, not meeting anyone's eyes that Eric could tell. He raised his mug and took another swig, then set out down with a *thunk*. "I need a day to wrap things up at my cabin. We'll leave day after tomorrow."

He pushed to his feet, his chair scraping as it moved backward. He gripped the rest of his biscuit in one hand and his empty plate in the other as he sent a tight smile to the women in the group. "Food was good. Thank you."

A few strides carried him to the work counter, where he plopped his plate in the bucket of wash water. Then his long legs carried him to the front door and out into the cold.

The door slapped shut behind him, leaving a tense quiet to settle in his wake.

CHAPTER 19

$\mathcal{N}$aomi's insides churned as she directed Anna to carry her plate and spoon and place them in the wash bucket. "Can you help Lillian and Angela bring more plates from the table?" Assisting with clean-up would help the girl feel like a part of them all.

Besides, Naomi desperately needed out of this cabin, and this way, Anna would be occupied and under Angela's watchful eyes. Naomi's tears were so close to the edge, they would escape her defenses soon, and she couldn't let that happen until she was alone. Eric was leaving. Again. He probably meant to return after searching in Fort Benton. But what if he didn't? What if something happened and he received an urgent summons from home? Or what if he simply changed his mind about how important she and Mary Ellen were to him?

"Let's get Sean's plate. I think he nearly licked it clean." Lillian rested a hand on Anna's shoulder to guide the girl back to the table.

Naomi slipped toward the front door while Anna was distracted. Dinah had taken Mary Ellen into Naomi's room to change her diaper. She would occupy her until Naomi returned.

Eric had gone outside with the rest of the men. Making plans for the trip, it sounded like.

Panic welled in Naomi's chest, and she grabbed her coat from the hook as she edged the door open and stepped out into the cold. The sun was bright again this morning, so the day would warm a little.

She turned toward the hidden trail to her little clearing. She needed to be alone. Needed a place to rid herself of these tears, then compose her mind, heart, and face before she returned to the others.

She'd just about reached the woods when a voice called from not too far behind her.

"Naomi." Her name in that deep voice always sent a ripple of warmth through her, but this time the ripple carried dread.

She couldn't face Eric now. Not yet.

But his footsteps crunched in the snow, and she stopped to wait for him to catch up.

When he reached her, she kept her face forward. Hopefully, her hood would conceal her red-rimmed eyes and splotchy cheeks.

"What's wrong?" His voice was laced with concern, his breath forming white clouds that lingered between them.

She walked again, her gaze fixed on the path ahead. She had to keep moving.

He matched her pace, staying at her side. "Are you worried about Jonah and me traveling together? Please don't fret. I'll do everything in my power to keep the peace."

A snort escaped before she could stop it. She shook her head. "You're both grown men. If you want to pummel each other, that's up to you."

They were almost to the clearing now. She could see the sunlight through the branches ahead.

Eric didn't speak again as they stepped into the open area.

The snow was mostly unbroken here, though several sets of small animal tracks crossed the white.

Eric's hand closed around her arm to halt her. Not a rough hold, but as firm as it was gentle. He turned her to face him. He could definitely see her face now. She wouldn't be able to hide from him. And maybe he needed to know the truth of her feelings.

His voice was rough, almost painful as he spoke. "What's wrong, Naomi? Please. Talk to me."

Her heart squeezed at the concern etched in his expression, the depths of sincerity in his eyes. She exhaled a breath. She needed to be able to share these things with him. "I can't bear the thought of you leaving." She glanced away. She didn't want this to feel like an accusation, not now that she knew he'd not abandoned her intentionally. But he needed to understand the pain she wrestled with.

"Every time I close my eyes, I see you walking away back in Wayneston. It might be irrational, but part of me fears that if you leave, you won't come back. I can't live through that pain again, Eric. Not again." Her voice broke on the last words, and her entire body shuddered.

Eric's gripped her arms, drawing her toward him. She resisted only a heartbeat, then let him pull her, giving in to his comfort. He wrapped his arms around her, and her tears surged past her barriers. As they streamed down her cheeks, she rested her head on his chest, letting his warmth soothe.

"I will come back to you, Naomi," he murmured. "To you and Mary Ellen. There's nothing on this earth that could keep me from returning to you." The rumble of his voice resonated in her ear, working its way deep inside her. Soothing the raw places bleeding inside her. This was what she needed. If he held her long enough, spoke these words enough times, she might believe them. The pain of the past would ebb away, replaced by the love surrounding her now.

He would come back to her. And...what? He'd said nothing yet about marriage. They hadn't had much time alone, not since that midnight kiss. What was he thinking for their future?

As if sensing her turmoil, Eric gently eased back, cradling her face in his hands. He lifted her chin so their eyes met—his so full of emotions. "I love you more than anything in this world. I want us to be the family we once dreamed we could be. Naomi Wyatt, will you marry me?" His voice was laced with a raw honesty that cut through her defenses, laying her soul bare.

Her heart swelled to the brink of bursting. Joy, pain, disbelief, and hope merged into a tumultuous storm within her. She had yearned for this moment, prayed for it during those long nights when the ache of his absence throbbed like an open wound. The emotions choked her, but through the tears, she found her voice—a whisper that carried the weight of her entire world. "Yes," she managed, the syllable laden with all the love and fear that warred in her heart.

His lips met hers then, in a kiss so tender it felt as if he were imprinting his promise onto her very soul. This wasn't the fiery kiss of passion they'd shared under the cover of darkness. It was a vow, a silent oath that spoke louder than words ever could.

Yet with her eyes closed and her face upturned, a memory slipped in. A reminder that she still had a secret from Eric. Could she stand to tell him what his cousin did? She had to. He deserved to know. But not now before he left. When he returned. Before they wed.

He lifted her face to look into her eyes, his own shimmering with a fierce determination that mirrored the resolve in his words. "I am coming back, Naomi. And when I do, we'll plan our wedding. I won't deny you the ceremony you deserve, but I also don't want to waste a single day without you as my wife. Our family...I want it to start as soon as we can manage."

His words made her heart yearn even more. She smiled at him. "I want that too."

He brushed a finger down her cheek. "We'll need to work out where we can live until the river thaws in the spring." He met her eyes. "I'll speak with Jericho to see what's best."

Unease niggled through her. "I'd like to stay here in these mountains. Maybe build a log cabin in one of the clearings near here." She glanced around. "Maybe this one in fact. We could cut a few more trees to make it larger." She sent him a hopeful smile. "We already have memories here."

His brows gathered, uncertainty marking his features. "We can talk more when I come back. I want you and Mary Ellen to be safe. And happy."

Then he pressed another kiss to her lips that stole every other thought.

* * *

Fort Benton at last.

Eric sat beside Jonah on the wagon bench as the other man skillfully guided the team around other rigs, riders, and pedestrians clogging the street. It'd been so long since he saw this many people at once, it felt almost like entering a strange country.

The journey here had actually turned out to be enjoyable. After a hearty send-off at the ranch, their first few days on the trail had been quiet, and civil. But not uncomfortable. At least, not after the first tense hour. Eric had made sure to do at least his share of the work, taking his turns driving the team and helping when they stopped to rest the animals to camp in the evenings.

Eric asked questions about the land they passed or the territory in general. As Jonah answered, the wealth of knowledge he possessed became clear, as well as his instinctual wisdom. The man had a good head on his shoulders, and even better, he possessed a dry humor that Eric enjoyed.

This last week of their trip, he actually enjoyed the days, seeing the landscape they traveled through and learning from Jonah the skills that came so easily to the man.

Now that they'd reached Fort Benton, though, Eric had his work cut out for him.

Jonah reined the team to a stop outside the livery, and the sharp scents of hay and manure mingled with the dust in the air. As he set the brake, and secured the reins, Eric climbed down from the rig. "You sure you don't want me to stay and help with the animals?"

Jonah stood and jumped from the step to the ground. "Nah. Go get your wire sent before Nash closes the mercantile. Irish'll help me." He spoke the last part as a man with a bushy head of red hair stepped into the sunlight.

He grinned a gap-toothed smile as he strode to the horses' heads. "It'd be my pleasure. 'Tis not often I get to stable beauties like these."

Eric grabbed the satchel that held his clothes and what few belongings he'd brought. "I'll head off then. See you at the hotel."

He'd spent two nights in Fort Benton when he first arrived on the steamer, and he remembered the route to Nash's mercantile easily enough. Just one street over. The sun had already turned the western sky into a brilliant canvas of blue and purple and pink, so the shop would likely be closing soon. Eric had already written out the message to his father. This errand should be quick enough.

As he crossed the final street, a call sounded from his right. "Eric? Eric LaGrange!"

The voice made him stop as much as hearing his name called. That sounded like Harvey, but it couldn't be. Not out here.

He turned...and took in the familiar figure striding toward him, half trotting.

He started toward his cousin, and they met on the boardwalk between the hotel and the mercantile. Harvey paused to catch his breath.

"What in the world are you doing all the way out here?" Eric asked.

It was surreal, seeing his well-dressed in this frontier town. Most of the men passing by on the street were clad in buckskins and fur coats.

Harvey, on the other hand, wore a wool coat unbuttoned to reveal his suit and string tie. He was clean-shaven as always, with long sideburns and pomade securing every hair in place. He'd freeze out here if he didn't get a better coat with a hood.

Harvey straightened and squared his shoulders, meeting Eric's gaze with pleasure, but also a sadness that made tension knot in Eric's middle.

"What's wrong?" His cousin wouldn't have traveled all this way unless something awful had happened. "Is it the Carson account? Did they decide to pull?" That was their largest client, and Eric had been the one to finalize the negotiations last year while his father was out recovering from the procedure on his knee.

In fact, the Carson account was the reason Eric had been gone from Naomi for so long that she'd given up on his coming back. His father's leg hadn't healed the way it should have, and Marcus Carson seemed to prefer dealing with Eric, even more than with his father. Eric had managed to move the discussions along farther than Dad ever had, with Carson finally signing the contract and nearly doubling the revenue *and* profits of LaGrange Exports. If Dad had ruined all his work by running Carson off...

But Harvey shook his head, his face sobering. "It's your dad. He's...he's dying."

A block rammed into Eric's chest, knocking the air from his lungs and all thought from his mind.

His father? Dying?

"He took ill right after you left. Aunt Mary thought it was just a bad cold with a little bit of fever. But when the doctor came, he said pneumonia had taken hold. He treated him, but his breathing grew worse. Another physician came, he said he has galloping consumption. It's drowning his lungs." Harvey took a step forward, sorrow pooling in his eyes, and gripped Eric's shoulder. "He only has three or four months left."

Eric's mind turned numb, his body too heavy to move.

Harvey's words repeated over and over. His father? Dying? It was impossible to reconcile. Dad had always been so healthy, so proud of being *in his prime, even at the youthful age of two-and-fifty,* as he always said.

The surgery the year before had been the only time he'd needed a doctor as far back as Eric could remember. His recovery had been slower than he'd expected, but he *had* recovered.

How could he have only four months to live? The doctor must be wrong. He had to be.

Eric had to see his father. Speak with the physician. Find a new one, a better one. A doctor who knew the difference between a cold and consumption. Between a hale and hearty man and an invalid at death's door.

"I need to get home. To help him." As the words left his mouth, an image of Naomi slipped into his mind. Those red, pain-filled eyes when she said she was afraid that if he left, he'd never come back.

He'd *promised her* he would return.

He'd not specified that he would come straight back from Fort Benton, but both of them knew that was what he meant.

If he traveled east now—for two and a half months, then stayed away however long he needed to make sure his father received the proper care...

The river would freeze.

No way he could get back before it thawed come spring. Early summer at best.

Naomi would be devastated.

But surely she would understand. If her father were dying, Eric would do everything possible to make sure she could be there with him.

A twinge pressed through the numbness in his chest.

When they'd first courted, more than a year and a half before, she'd not seen her parents in years. Their only correspondence was an annual birthday card as they continued their work in New York. She'd said they spent their days advocating for the rights of all who lived in America, regardless of what race or country they hailed from. A noble cause, to be sure, but how could they possibly put other people's needs so far ahead of those of their two remarkable daughters?

Naomi had never talked much about them, but the few times she had, he'd seen the depth of her pain in her eyes. She would certainly understand this urgent need to be there when his parents needed him most.

Maybe she could go with him. His heart jumped at the idea. She and Mary Ellen could go east with him, and he could introduce his daughter to her grandparents.

But it would take a month to get back to Naomi and gather the two of them. The river would be frozen. How would they ever get east? Whatever the means of travel, it would likely be too dangerous. Far too risky to subject his girls to. Not to mention cold.

Harvey was talking, and Eric had to focus. "I knew you'd realize you needed to come, assuming if I could ever find you. We tried to reach you by telegraph, but no one in that Missoula Mills town you gave us knew who you were. I finally decided I had to come myself. Got here a few days ago, and I've been trying to figure out how to locate you. This place is as backward as a blacksmith at a ladies' tea. And the people..."

Eric held up his hand to stop the flow. He couldn't listen to his cousin demean the land he'd come to appreciate so well. Besides, they needed to make plans. "You came on a steamer?"

Harvey launched into a diatribe about the horrible conditions he'd dealt with.

"So the river's not frozen yet?" Eric interrupted the man's complaints. He'd forgotten how fussy Harvey could be. "We'd thought it might be since the snowstorm."

Harvey's expression turned sour. "It is. Seems the whole place is cut off from civilization. The boat I came in on was the last one that made it. In fact, we had to disembark a mile downriver because the captain feared the ice would break through his hull. We waited ages in the cold and wind for them to bring transportation. You'd think they'd be prepared, but it was like they'd never done the like before. And then it was wagons of all things. Not even a single coach. I've never been jostled so much in all my life."

Eric wanted to grip his cousin's shoulders and shake him till he stopped talking. He couldn't think straight with all that griping. "Be quiet a minute. I need to think."

Was there any way to travel on the river with it iced over? Or could they rent a rig and travel overland? It'd be cheaper and easier just to buy horses. Maybe a few weeks on horseback would be good for Harvey. Turn his blisters into calluses so he'd toughen up some.

Eric had to talk to Jonah. He would know the best way to travel.

CHAPTER 20

*E*ric spun, scanning the street for him. No sign among the passersby, so he started back toward the livery.

"Where are you going?" Harvey called from behind.

Eric glanced back to make sure he was coming too. "I need to find my friend. He'll know how to travel with the river frozen." *Friend.* After these past weeks on the trail, the label felt right.

Harvey caught up with him, following close as Eric wove through the horse and wagon traffic on the side-street that led to the main road and livery. As they turned the corner, he nearly bumped into Jonah.

They both lurched to a stop, and Harvey stepped on Eric's heel as he realized the change in pace too late.

Jonah frowned. "What's wrong?"

Anxiety thrummed through Eric's veins. "It's my father." He stepped to the side to reveal Harvey. "This is my cousin, Harvey Reynolds. He came looking for me. My father's ill. The doctor said maybe only a few months left. How can I get back east to a train station? Is there a way to travel on the ice?" Probably not, but he had to ask.

Jonah's frown deepened, and Eric could see worry churning in his eyes. "Horseback is the only option that makes sense. It's not easy, especially in the snow. You can count on bad weather for some of it. If you hit a snowstorm on the prairie..." He shook his head. "It's too hard." A harder shake, as though he'd made up his mind. "No. That's not a good option."

Panic welled in Eric's chest. "What else then? My father is dying. At least that's what the doctor said. I'm sure someone else could help him though. I have to get there. They need me." He sucked in a breath. He needed to help with the business too. Who was managing it while his father was ill? And if the worst happened...

Jonah gave another slow shake of his head. "Your only decent option would be to hire someone to take you. A guide who knows how to survive when the weather gets rough." His brows stayed low, his expression troubled.

A guide? Maybe that would be best. As much as Jonah learned on his way to and from the ranch, he might not be aware of a critical step in helping them survive a snowstorm without shelter.

Could Jonah...? No, he wouldn't ask this man to leave his family for weeks. Months.

He met the man's gaze. "Who would you suggest?" Though the Coulters lived far from Fort Benton, they seemed to know people here.

Jonah pressed his lips together, considering for a moment before he responded. "There's a man. Silas Grant. He's rough around the edges, but he has a reputation for knowing this land and how to manage it. He's guided folks through worse winters than this." He offered a wry smile. " I just saw him in the livery, coming in from a scouting trip. Don't know if he has his next ride lined up, so you might want to get to him before anyone else does."

Eric's muscles tensed. "Thank you." He moved around Jonah. "I'll catch up with you at the hotel when I can."

Harvey stayed on his heels as Eric strode across the street and a few doors down to the livery.

Inside, Irish was talking to a man draped in animal furs. A few even had the stuffed heads still intact—muskrat or fox maybe, though Eric was no expert on local wildlife.

When that fellow turned at Eric and Harvey's approach, his beard drew Eric's gaze more than anything else. Long and white, it nearly blended into the pale tan-and-white fur across his chest. Between his beard and the fur cap on his head, the man's eyes were too shadowed to make out well.

Eric met his gaze with a friendly nod. "I'm looking for Silas Grant. Might you be him?" Seemed a good guess. This fellow looked more than capable of surviving in a mountain snowstorm—or any other disaster that dared face off against him.

The man's eyes, dark and piercing, assessed Eric for a moment before he spoke. "I know a Silas Grant. What business do you have with him."

Eric had been in more than one negotiation with a shrewd and skeptical businessman. This likely was Silas, and he simply needed to know Eric meant no harm. That in fact what Eric had to say would be a help to him. That was what usually drew a man into a more open mindset for negotiations.

Eric offered a friendly expression. "I've heard he's the best guide around. I need to get back east. I just received word my father is dying and my family needs me there. I've plenty of respect for this land and would appreciate if Silas would consider being our guide—as far east as he'd like to go, or until we reach a stretch that would be safe for us to travel alone." He gave a deferential nod. "We'd be willing to pay whatever he felt the work was worth." Surely a guide's services, horses, and supplies wouldn't cost much more than the three hundred dollar steamer ride he'd planned for his return trip. He had extra in case he needed it. And Harvey wouldn't have come empty-handed.

Speaking of... He stepped to the side so Silas could see his cousin. "My cousin and I will be traveling. I'm Eric LaGrange, and this is Harvey Reynolds."

The man's assessing gaze hadn't shifted while Eric spoke. Maybe he should have been short and to the point. *Need a guide to go east.* But he'd figured Silas wanted enough detail to decide if this was a project he wanted to take on.

At last, Silas gave a single dip of his chin. "I 'spose I can do it. When you headed out?"

Relief eased through Eric, but he tried not to show it. "Tomorrow morning would be good. Or as soon as you're ready."

The man still eyed him as though trying to read him. Was this simply his thinking expression? Or had Silas still not settled in his mind that he'd take the job?

It must be the former, for Silas's next words were, "I'll order supplies at McCracken's. Go by an' pay the tab afore we leave at daylight."

Eric nodded. "Sounds like a good plan." That would keep him from guessing at what they'd need.

Silas turned away, and Eric finally looked at Harvey. His cousin eyes were wide and a little twitchy.

He motioned for Harvey to follow him out. He could ease his cousin's worries by sharing how fortunate they were to find a guide such as Silas. The wisdom of experience might well save their lives during one of these winter storms.

After that, he needed to send a telegram to his parents before that office closed, secure horses for them, and find Jonah to share their plans.

Jonah would have to be the one to tell Naomi why he'd gone. Would he use the opportunity to his advantage? It was hard to say. Eric had come to respect the man, but there had certainly been that earlier rivalry. And Eric had not announced his and Naomi's engagement, so Jonah wouldn't see her as off limits.

Eric should tell him tonight. But he hated to part with bad blood between them. They'd both been careful to keep from mentioning Naomi or Mary Ellen.

Besides, he trusted Naomi. She could reveal their engagement to the others if she chose, and he had no doubt she would save her heart for him.

The best thing would be to write her a letter for Jonah to deliver. Surely, he'd carry out that one request. He was an honorable man.

Eric would do everything he could to ensure Naomi would be at peace until he returned, then he'd have to leave the outcome in God's hands.

A niggle of unrest churned inside him. He'd done that before, a year and a half before. And look how things had turned out. But he didn't have any other choice this time.

* * *

"*A*nd God blessed Noah and his sons, and said unto them, 'Be fruitful, and multiply, and replenish the earth.'" Naomi shifted her finger to the next line of small type in the Bible.

At her feet, Anna had Mary Ellen occupied with the abacus, and on either side of her, Lillian and Sean worked on their usual projects to occupy their hands while she read. Sean was chipping away at his block of wood to form legs for a horse, and Lillian was stitching closed a hole on her uncle Gil's shirt. That man had a knack for snagging his clothing on branches or the sharp point of a cow's horn.

Naomi pressed on to the next chapter. "And the fear of you and the dread of you shall—" A squeal from the rug drew her attention from the page.

"Let me have it." Anna's voice held a playful yet firm tone as she reached for the bead necklace Mary Ellen held away from her. "That's mine. You play with your beads." Anna nudged the abacus back in front of the tot.

Naomi leaned forward to help. That necklace had been Anna's grandmother's, and the girl treasured it. The beads were wooden, brightly painted with intricate designs. From the few pieces of clothing and accessories Gammy had with her, the woman seemed to have a penchant for color and fun patterns. She probably would have been a delight to know.

Before Naomi could grab her daughter's hand and ease the necklace from her, Mary Ellen dropped it and reached for the abacus.

"You're such a good baby." Anna patted her head with a satisfied smile.

Naomi couldn't help her own smile. Anna was so good with her daughter, almost like a little mother. She would make a wonderful big sister. And Mary Ellen adored her, often complying with something Anna asked, when she usually would have pitched a fit at being told no. Like just now with the necklace.

Naomi turned her gaze back to the Bible, but a memory swept through her—a moment from the dream she'd had the night before. Jonah had returned driving a fully-loaded wagon up the mountainside. And he'd been alone. She'd run to him, clutching the wagon's side. Before she could ask about Eric, he shook his head sadly. He said Eric decided that, since he was so close to home, he would keep going all the way back to Washington D.C. Jonah said Eric told him he would be back for Naomi someday. But even as Jonah said those last words, a voice rose up in the distance, booming laughter. In her dream, she'd somehow known that laughter was Eric's, laughing that she might believe he'd ever return.

She blinked hard to force the nightmare from her mind.

Each dream seemed to get worse, and they came at least every other night. Was God trying to tell her something? He'd used dreams in the Bible sometimes to warn people.

These dreams didn't feel like Heavenly messages exactly. They felt melodramatic and hopeless. But still...

A weight pressed on her shoulders, wrapping around her chest. Should she be worried about Eric? He and Jonah had been gone a little over two weeks, so they should have arrived at Fort Benton by now, as long as the travel went well.

Lord, help them in their search. Help them learn of Anna's aunt. Give Eric wisdom. And bring him back to me. Both of them. Please, God, bring Eric back to me. The more she prayed, the more desperate her heart became. If Eric didn't come back...

She squeezed her eyes closed, searching for the peace that usually came when she prayed. *Give me wisdom, too, Lord. Show me if I'm supposed to do anything.*

Yet what could she do? Going after him would be rash, especially since there was no reason to worry. None save the turmoil inside her.

Show me what to do. Please.

CHAPTER 21

$\mathcal{T}$he icy morning air bit at Eric's exposed face as he stood beside Jonah outside the livery. Eric had finished saddling his new horse early and come out to say farewell to this man he'd never thought he would consider a friend.

The two of them stood quietly for a minute, watching the handful of early-bird frontiersmen trudge by on the street. Harvey and Silas would step from the livery any minute, so Eric didn't have much time to say what needed saying.

His breath clouded in the morning air as he released it. "I'm sorry I'm leaving you to search the passenger lists alone." The guilt pressed once more. "It's not that I think finding Anna's aunt isn't important..."

Jonah waved the concern away. "Your pa is sick. You need to get there as quick as you can." One corner of his mouth lifted in a sad smile. "If my dat were alive, I'd wanna be near him too."

Eric nodded, the thought of losing his father pressing down on him. "My mother's reply to my wire made it sound like my father is weakening at the rate the doctors expected. They still think he only has two or three months left." She'd said they'd called in two other physicians too. The situation must really be as bad as Harvey said.

"We'll be praying for you all." Jonah's voice was earnest, his eyes kind.

Eric worked for a smile. "Thank you. I'll be back to Montana as soon as I can. I just need to take care of things for my parents."

Jonah's gaze shifted to the street. He didn't say anything for a long time.

Did he *wish* Eric would stay away? That he would hand over Naomi? Not until Eric's last breath could he ever do that.

When Jonah did speak, his words gave no sign of what he'd been thinking. "Anyway, I'll do everything I can with the search. If there's a record on file showing a Patsy or Patty or Patricia came through here in the last two years, I'll find it." He tipped a friendly smile at Eric.

Eric met his gaze and made sure the truth of his words sounded in his voice. "Thank you. For everything."

Jonah held the look, his eyes impossible to read. Was he weighing Eric's sincerity? He seemed to think about something.

At last, he straightened. "I guess it needs to be said. You don't need to worry about me with Naomi while you're gone. I won't try to step into your place or win her back. She made her choice, and I'll respect that." One side of his mouth tipped up. "Can't promise I won't tickle that little girl o' yours, but I'll make sure she knows I'm just Uncle Jonah."

Was that a flash of pain in his eyes? If moved away so fast that Eric couldn't tell.

Jonah's gaze shifted past Eric to somewhere in the distance. "I knew she didn't love me when I asked her to marry me. I just wanted to give her and Mary Ellen a good life." His focus flashed back to Eric, and this time his eyes turned intense. His voice was almost stern when he spoke. "I sure do hope you'll give her that good life she deserves. Both of them."

Eric's chest tightened. "I will. No matter what." With everything in him, until his last breath.

Jonah's words must have been hard to say, and certainly not many men would have thought them worth the effort. He searched for the best way to acknowledge that. He extended a hand. "You're a good man, Jonah Coulter. One of the very best."

Jonah met his with a firm clasp. "Go with God."

As Eric released Jonah's hand, Silas emerged from the livery, leading a mount and a packhorse piled high.

Harvey straggled behind their guide, leading his horse and looking far too much the dandy in his three-piece suit.

Eric settled into his saddle as the others did, raising a chorus of creaking leather as the horses shifted restlessly.

He raised a hand in farewell to Jonah as Silas started forward. Jonah offered the same, but then Eric's horse started forward behind the pack animal, and he had to turn forward to focus on riding.

As they passed wooden storefronts on the way out of town, he tried to settle into the rhythm of the ride. He was comfortable enough on a horse, and this one seemed mannerly enough.

Yet there was an unsettled feeling in his chest... Was it only the discomfort of goodbyes? It felt like more than that. Like something was very wrong, and he needed to find out what.

But of course something was wrong—his father was dying, according to the doctor. Also, he couldn't stop worry about leaving Naomi without knowing for sure she understood. Hopefully his letter would explain the situation to her satisfaction. He'd poured his heart out to her. Made promises he would keep if his life depended on it.

He'd done everything he could. If there was anything else wrong, only God could do anything about it now.

* * *

*N*aomi awoke in the darkness, her heart pounding as the remnants of her dream clung to her like an icy mist. The morning light coming through the window was still barely more than darkness. She should get up and start coffee and the morning meal.

But as she slipped quietly into her shoes and wrapped a shawl around her, the desperation from the dream pressed like a weight.

This had been different from the others.

She saw Eric as though looking down at him from the sky. He rode between two other men, away from Fort Benton, away from the mountains. Toward the east.

She couldn't tell who the two other men were. But then a voice spoke, deep and resonant. It had been Jonah's voice, or at least that was what she'd thought in the dream. His words...

She sucked in a breath as they resounded in her heart now.

If you really choose Eric, you'd better go after him.

She stepped into the main room and eased the bed chamber door shut behind her, breathing out a prayer. *Show me what to do.*

No voice boomed around her, like in her dream. Nor a quiet whisper in her mind.

She headed toward the cookstove and her morning ritual. She needed to build up the fire .

As she worked through each familiar task, her mind strayed through one awful possibility after another. Maybe Eric really had decided to go east. Why, though? Was it the roughness of the trail to Fort Benton, sleeping in the cold for two weeks? Perhaps he'd simply missed the comforts of civilization. Had she scared him off when she said she'd like to stay here in the mountains? He hadn't seemed to like the idea, but surely he would come back and talk through things with her. Once he saw how important this land had become to her, how peaceful and inspiring the mountains were, he would feel the same.

Maybe he'd received a telegram from his father, begging him to come back to the business. Or maybe commanding him. Was Mr. LaGrange the kind of man to give an ultimatum—get back to your work or you're through here?

Would Eric give in to such an ultimatum?

The door to Dinah and Jericho's room opened, and Jericho emerged, stretching his broad shoulders as he moved towards the door leading outside. His face softened when he saw Naomi by the stove, and with a gesture that was both habitual and comforting, he offered her a small wave accompanied by the words that signaled another day on the Coulter ranch. "Mornin', Naomi."

Naomi worked for a normal tone. "Good morning, Jericho."

A few minutes after the door closed behind him, Dinah stepped out of the room, her long hair in a fresh braid and her expression filled with the softness of sleep.

She approached the kitchen area and patted Naomi's shoulder as she reached for an apron to begin her usual tasks. "How did you sleep?"

Dinah's question was innocent enough. A casual greeting the went barely deeper than if she'd said, *Good morning*. But it was too close to the mark, and Naomi couldn't bear up under this weight much longer. Maybe Dinah would know what to do.

She stopped stirring the johnny cake batter but kept her hands on the spoon and the bowl. "I keep having these dreams. I don't know what they mean."

Dinah must have caught the tension in her voice, for she halted her work, turning to face Naomi with a scoop of flour in one hand. "Tell me."

Naomi swallowed. Did she dare? Dinah might think her batty. Or love-sick. They'd not had one of their girl nights in so long. How long had it been since she'd confided a secret to her sister?

She could trust Dinah though. If anyone would listen without judging, her twin would.

"They're always about Eric not coming back. Usually it's Jonah showing up here with a full wagon and no Eric. He says Eric decided to go back east since he was so close."

Worry drew Dinah's brows close and clouded her eyes. But she didn't say anything, so Naomi continued.

"Last night's was a little different. And...worse." Her breathing came hard just thinking about it. "I saw Eric riding away from Fort Benton with two other men. Then I heard Jonah's voice saying that if I really chose Eric, I'd better go after him."

Her pulse surged through her chest. "I don't know what's happening, Dinah, but something's wrong. Yesterday when I was reading to the children, I had this overwhelming panic that came out of nowhere. It was like dread just settled over me, and I knew something wasn't right with Eric."

Dinah's eyes glistened, and she set the flour down, grabbed Naomi's shoulders and pulled her in for a hug. "Oh, Naomi."

Naomi couldn't let herself cry, not when the men would come in any minute. And crying would not help her know what to do.

She rested her hands at Dinah's back for a few seconds, then pulled back, fortifying herself with a deep breath. She squared her gaze in her sister's. "What should I do? I can't carry on here as if nothing's wrong. *Something* is wrong."

Dinah swallowed. "Have you prayed? Has God given you any insight?"

A thread of hopelessness wove its way through her. "I've prayed. Mostly for Eric, but also for me. I can't hear Him saying anything, though."

Certainty changed Dinah's expression, and she reached for Naomi's hands. "Let's pray now."

Naomi let her hands be enveloped by her twins, and they

bowed their heads, the warmth from their clasped fingers spreading through her like a balm.

"Heavenly Father," Dinah began, her voice steady like a beacon in the storm that raged within Naomi's soul. "We come before You with troubled hearts. You know Naomi's dreams, her fears for Eric and for their future. We ask now for Your wisdom to guide her. Lord, show us the path she should take and calm her spirit with Your unending grace."

The words washed over Naomi, soothing the jagged edges of her fear. They stood like that for several moments in silence, and she sank into the peace from Naomi's prayer. Peace from God, actually.

Finally, Dinah opened her eyes and gave Naomi's hands a squeeze. "Sometimes, clarity comes in unexpected moments."

Naomi nodded, then turned back to her work. "The men will be here soon. I'd rather not face them without food and coffee ready."

If Dinah hadn't been here, Naomi's absent mind would have scorched the coffee and all the johnny cakes, but together they got the food ready and all the family around the table. Though Dinah's prayer had brought a measure of peace, the unrest inside her wouldn't settle. It wasn't so much worry now, but an awful churning in her middle.

Something was wrong, and she couldn't let it rest.

Finally, the others finished eating, and the men filed out to finish the morning's outside chores and saddle their horses for the day's work. Dinah and Lillian started on the dishes, and Angela offered to take Mary Ellen and Anna outside for a few minutes.

Naomi should offer to go with them. Angela could handle the children fine on her own, but the kitchen wasn't large enough for three bodies at the wash bucket, and she should do something useful. Maybe the children could distract her.

But her gaze wandered to the window, and her feet followed

along. Through the small square, she studied the activity near the barn. Miles throwing hay to the horses who would stay in the corral today.

Two riders appeared at the edge of the woods, riding toward the barn. The moment Naomi recognized them, her heart quickened.

She must have gasped, for Dinah called from behind. "What is it?"

"Two Stones and Heidi. I wonder what they're doing out so early." And why did their appearance make her pulse race. Was she simply on edge?

"Invite them in for coffee and food." The scrape of metal sounded as Dinah moved the pot to the warm part of the stove.

Naomi headed for the door. When she pulled it open, several of the men had gathered around the couple.

Naomi waved to catch their attention.

Heidi turned her horse toward the house. They must be riding through, not planning to dismount. Where were they going?

As Heidi neared, Naomi lifted her voice. "Can you come in for coffee and food?"

Heidi gave a polite shake of her head as she reined in beside the stoop. "We need to keep moving. Just stopped in to let you all know we're headed to Fort Benton. Two Stones wanted to do one more supply run before winter sets in. Is there anything you need?"

Naomi's heart lurched, her pulse racing. "Fort Benton?" This was it. This was her chance to do as Jonah had said in the dream. She gripped the door frame for support. "Can I come with you?"

Heidi pulled back in surprise. "Really? Why?" She shook her head. "I mean, are you sure? It won't be an easy journey. Two Stones thinks it might snow in the next few days."

"I'm certain." She would brave a couple weeks in the snow and cold to stop whatever awful thing was happening with Eric.

But Mary Ellen...

She spun to find her sister, but Dinah was already right behind her. "Dinah, can you watch Mary Ellen and Anna while I'm gone? I know it's a lot to ask, but I *have* to find Eric. Something isn't right, and I really think God is telling me to go—especially since He brought Two Stones and Heidi here for me to travel with."

Concern etched across her sister's face, her eyes dark and troubled. She looked outside, maybe for Jericho, then met Naomi's gaze. "Of course, I'll take care of the children. But..."

Naomi waited, her middle churning so much she worried that bile might force its way up her throat soon.

At last, Dinah said, "Let's talk to Jericho. He might have some wisdom about how best to proceed."

Naomi eased out a breath. "All right. But let's hurry."

CHAPTER 22

"*I* don't know why it has to be so blasted windy out here."

Eric forced himself not to acknowledge Harvey's complaining. It wouldn't change his cousin's outlook nor stop his endless whining. And it had been harder and harder these past three days on the trail to keep from spouting off to put Harvey in his place, which would strike at a deep hurt. Pain that probably only Eric knew, because he'd been there to witness how five-year-old Harvey had cried after his father's insults.

Though that word—*insult*—was too shallow for the things Oliver Reynolds had said to his son.

And Eric couldn't bring himself to even allude to them.

Besides, he should be grateful Harvey came all this way to tell him about his father's condition. He'd risked his life for this.

Another gust of wind swept through, whipping the flaps of his coat and pelting his face with tiny ice fragments that felt like sand. He ducked his chin and squinted to protect his eyes. This open plain stretched as far as he could see, only a few low rises breaking the flat expanse. No wonder the wind explored freely through here.

Something flashed in front of his eyes. Snowflakes? Two white crystals fell onto his horse's neck, a little bigger than sand and floating far lazier than solid ice would do. Silas had mentioned snow would come soon when they were saddling the horses that morning. So far, the man had not been wrong in any of his predictions and suggestions.

Eric glanced over at him, riding on his left and pulling ahead a little. Thank the Lord Jonah had recommended him.

"Of all the lousy…" Harvey's voice carried that grating whiny tone. "It's snowing. Get me out of this godforsaken…"

Eric did his best to block out the rest of his cousin's complaints.

Silas, apparently, had reached the end of his patience. He swung around to glare at Harvey. "How exactly do you propose I do that? You want me to conjure up a cabin out here on the plain? Snap my fingers and make up some trees for the wood? Or maybe you'd like me to blink and send you back to whatever high-brow city house you came from where people wait on ya hand an' foot. Believe me, Pilgrim, I'd like ta do it. Fer now though, there ain't no way I can be shed of ya. So I'd appreciate it if ye'd keep yer complainin' confined to her head an' try not to sour the trip for the rest of us."

Eric would have smiled if his cheeks weren't frozen stiff. He couldn't have said it better himself.

Harvey grumbled a response, but it wasn't loud enough to make out, so maybe he'd picked up on the lesson.

Silas turned forward again, and he stepped a little quicker, dragging the pack horse behind him. "We need to push harder. Maybe we can make it to shelter before dark. Else we'll have to make our own."

Silas didn't need a response, so Eric didn't work to offer one. The man seemed to appreciate a nice stretch of silence. Though anytime Eric asked a question—about the land around them, the animals in the area, or even his experiences as a guide—Silas answered readily, giving plenty of detail and usually a story or two thrown in. He didn't use flowery words to set the scene, but the few descriptors he offered made his tales spring to life in vivid detail.

Just now, it would be nice if Silas could tell a story about a warm summer day so they could at least imagine they weren't pushing through an icy wind that pelted them with more and more icy flakes with every gust.

Within a few minutes, the small flakes turned into a flurry of white, whipping sideways, and somehow still landing to blanket the ground in an uneven layer.

Harvey's horse stumbled.

His cousin shouted, and the animal lurched forward as it tried to regain its footing.

Eric jerked his own gelding toward his cousin. "Hold his head up!" His mouth was so numb, the words slurred out of him.

It was too late anyway. Harvey clutched his saddle with both hands, and the horse steadied itself, limping forward a few steps before slowing to a halt.

Worry tightened Eric's chest as he stopped his mount beside his cousin. Silas had already dismounted and moved to the mare's head. "Get down so I can check her."

Harvey's face wore a thick scowl as he slid to the ground, but at least he kept his words to himself.

Eric also dismounted in case there was anything he could do to help. Silas shucked his gloves and crouched beside the mare's front left leg, running his red hands down from her shoulder to hoof. As he worked, Eric glance back to the spot the horse had stumbled. The ground was darker where her hooves had cleared the snow, but he couldn't tell what had tripped her.

He left his gelding standing with the others and walked back to the area. One particular dark spot made a knot twist in his belly.

A hole. He didn't poke his foot into the opening, but it looked at least as deep as the length of his forearm. Made by some burrowing creature, no doubt.

He strode back to Silas as he rose and patted the mare's shoulder. "She stepped in a hole," Eric said. "A deep one."

"Yup." Silas nodded. "Ankle's already swelling and warm to the touch." He let out a sigh as he straightened and scanned the land around them. "It'd be better to let her rest now an' see if she'll heal. If we push her right off, we'll likely be down a horse in less than a day."

He turned toward his pack horse. "Best we can do is make a tent an' settle in."

While Harvey unloaded the animals, Eric helped Silas stretch out the canvas he'd folded at the bottom of his supplies. Then they built a low but wide tent using an extendable pole he'd tucked away, as well as some of the dry firewood the pack-horse carried in case they needed to start a fire in the rain or snow. Once more, Silas was proving more valuable than any amount of gold.

Once they'd settled the horses as best they could, the three of them tucked under the covering. Silas nurtured a fire while Eric and Harvey stretched out bedding. With the canvas so low above them, it would be easier to lie than sit while they waited.

With his body finally still, it didn't take long for his mind to churn with worries. This was only their third day on the trail, and they were already delayed. Silas had hoped they'd reach the settlements with regular roads and lodging in about a month and a half. Did that take into account extended stops like this one?

He glanced at the guide, still crouched over his low flame. Could he present the question in a way that didn't sound like Harvey's griping? He'd have to try, for he needed to know the answer. The urgency in his chest pressed so much harder when they weren't making progress. His father could die before he even reached him.

He summoned his most reasonable tone. "I know it's hard to see the future, but do you expect this will slow us down from that month and a half you were thinking?"

Silas didn't look his way, and he paused before answering. "Like you said, it's hard to see the future."

Eric let out a breath but did his best not to allow a groan to escape. This wasn't Silas's fault, so he couldn't hold him accountable for the lost time. Nor could he expect him to be a fortune teller.

He let his eyes close. *God, let the snow stop and the horse heal. We need to make up time. And help my father. Keep him alive until I can get there. Please.*

* * *

As Naomi rode beside Heidi and Two Stones on the road toward Fort Benton, she studied the wagon that had just crested the hill ahead of them. They were still about three days from Fort Benton, but those horses...the familiar and solid form of the driver. That was definitely Jonah.

And there was no passenger. Unless Eric was lying down in the back.

She forced air in through the pressure on her chest. This was just like her dream. She pushed her mount faster. The mare obliged, moving into a trot, then pushing to a lope. She must feel Naomi's tension.

But she couldn't make her body relax.

Why would Eric not come back? Had he found information about Anna's aunt and decided to search for her in one of the towns?

If that was the case, why wouldn't Jonah to go with him?

Maybe the place was too remote. Jonah might not want to

carry his precious glass windows over too many extra miles or terrain too treacherous.

Jonah lifted a hand in greeting but didn't speak.

She reined in beside him as he halted the team and wagon, setting the brake.

Her mouth was too dry to speak. By Jonah's grim expression, he understood her question. He pulled a folded paper out of his chest pocket as he spoke. "Eric got word his father's ill. Dying, he said. He and his cousin set off with a guide to try to make it east before his father passes."

He held out the paper for her, but her mind was too numb to process more than his words.

He'd gone east. Just like in her dream.

Her nightmare. But for his father? His father dying? Did he think he'd get there in time? Or was he going to be with his mother? How long would he be gone? Did he ever intend to come back? Even if he planned to, how many hundreds of duties would hold him there?

"You said his cousin was with him?" Concern laced Heidi's voice. "Did he come to find Eric?"

Naomi glanced at her friend as she struggled to make sense of those questions.

His cousin? What was she talking about? The only cousin Eric had was…the one she didn't let herself think about. But what in the cloudy sky did he have to do with this?

"He was in Fort Benton when we rode in." Jonah's words made no sense. "Said he came on the last steamer before the river froze. He came to get Eric and take him back to try to reach his father before the end." Jonah waved the paper a little. "I think Eric explained it all in the letter he wrote for you."

Bile churned in Naomi's middle as she eyed the missive.

Harvey was here.

Harvey was involved.

Anything that involved Harvey could only be awful news.

Was he telling the truth about Eric's father? Or simply trying to get Eric away from her, to lure him back under the guise of tragedy and family responsibility.

She snatched the letter, but her gloved hands trembled, and she fumbled the page, nearly crinkling it before she final unfolded the flaps.

My Darling,

I'm so grieved as I write this, torn between my promise and desire to return to you with all speed and the grief of learning my father is ill. More than ill, if one can believe the physician. Mere months from death. I can't credit it. My father has always been the picture of health and was so when I left him last summer. That a lung condition could slay him so quickly seems impossible. Nevertheless, I'm needed at his side. Either to find a doctor able to treat whatever malady truly ails him, or to comfort my mother as she loses the rock she's depended on for nearly two score years.

My cousin Harvey brought the news to me, coming in person when they couldn't locate me by telegram. His steamship was the last to paddle the Missouri before the final freeze, so we have hired a guide to help us travel east by horse. I know the journey will hold its challenges, but I cannot delay a single day.

If the worst happens, I'm sure I will be needed to handle arrangements and settle matters with the business also, and I pray I can find competent hands in which to leave it. But rest assured, my love, I will return to you and our daughter the moment I am able. We will have that wedding we spoke of, and my name will be yours forever, just as my heart is in full already.

Give our sweet Mary Ellen a big hug for me and tell her Papa misses her and will be back as soon as he can.

Yours always,

Eric

The words blurred behind the tears that she finally stopped fighting. *Eric. Oh, Eric.*

She squeezed her eyes shut against the wrenching in her chest. The awful knife piercing through gashes that had only just healed over.

He'd left her. Even admitting how very much he loved her, he'd left.

And Harvey—once again—was the villain driving the wedge between them with an iron mallet.

God, why?

Her heart screamed the question. Hadn't she and Eric learned from last time? They'd not allowed an indiscretion this time. They'd kept themselves chaste. Why were they being punished again? She should have told him the truth about Harvey. None of this would be happening if she'd gathered her courage and been honest.

She sucked in a breath, still keeping her eyes closed. She had to control her emotions with the others around. A few tears could be overlooked, but she couldn't break down completely. That would have to wait until later.

For now... She forced her eyes open. Forced her mind to think about what she should do.

Heidi rested a hand on her shoulder, probably for comfort. Naomi needed to tell them her concerns about Harvey. She couldn't say why, but they could help decide the next step.

She turned and faced all three of them. "What Jonah said is right. Eric's cousin Harvey came to Fort Benton to find him and bring him back to Washington D.C. The river is frozen, so they hired a guide and left to travel over land." She inhaled a breath. "I know Harvey. I have had...past dealings with him." Her voice trembled a little, but she pressed on. "He can't be trusted. I'm not even certain the story about Mr. LaGrange's illness is true." Should she have said that aloud? Would it be disrespectful to Eric's father if he really was deathly sick? "I can't know, of course, but I do know Harvey is a danger. He's the reason Eric and I never received each other's letters back when he left Wayneston. Whatever he wants, it must be significant for him to come all this way to get Eric, then be willing to travel back on horseback through winter storms."

Had she explained the situation clearly? Her mind had formed such a muddle, she couldn't sort a clear plan.

"What are you saying?" Jonah demanded. "You think Eric's cousin would hurt him?"

She turned that question over in her mind. "I...I don't know if he'd hurt him physically. But he has something underhanded in the works. Something that will help him, no matter how badly it hurts other people."

Jonah's gaze narrowed, as though he was thinking hard.

Heidi said, "Eric surely knows this about his cousin, don't you think? He'll be cautious. Maybe he'll even turn around come back if he realizes Harvey concocted the entire scheme."

Fresh tears welled in her eyes. "That's the problem. Eric is blind to his cousin's evils. I tried to tell him before... I-I wish I'd told him everything. I should have. I just... I wish I'd let him see exactly how wicked that man is." Her voice rose with her words, but she couldn't control it. She'd worked hard to put what Harvey did behind her. But she'd *not* stand by and allow him to destroy a second time her chance for happiness with Eric.

She squared her shoulders. "I'm going after Eric. God warned me about this in dreams. He made it clear I'm to go after Eric and bring him back."

She gave the others a minute to respond. Surely Two Stones and Heidi would ride with her, at least to Fort Benton. They'd have to move faster though. She needed speed to catch up to him.

Heidi exchanged a look with Two Stones, but before either could speak a word, Jonah said. "I'll go with you." His tone was low. Absolutely certain.

She met his gaze, hoping he saw the gratitude in her eyes.

"Of course we will too," Heidi said.

She took in all three of them as she offered a weak smile. "Thank you."

Jonah nodded, then reached down to release the wagon's brake. "Let me turn the team and we'll head out."

CHAPTER 23

*E*ric squinted through the thick curtain of snow swirling around them. The biting wind found every crack in his clothing, burning his skin with stinging ice. The snow had piled up to the horses' knees, making each step a laborious effort for the animals.

Did Silas really plan to keep going in this? As much as Eric wanted to make up for lost time, this felt like madness.

The older man's face was set like stone, determination etched into the lines that framed his mouth and eyes. Yet even with all the years Silas had spent enduring Montana winters, he couldn't be immune to this agony.

Silas glanced his way and nodded as if conceding to the unspoken request. "We'll make camp in those trees."

Eric peered through the white to see what he meant. They'd not passed trees in hours—at least not that he'd seen.

It took a moment before he made out a dark form in the distance. That must be what Silas meant.

Relief sank through Eric.

At last they reached the stretch of woods, and when the

animals stepped under the canopy of pines, the wind instantly quieted, it's howl sounding distant.

Silas halted them a dozen strides in at a spot where the tree trunks spread farther apart, allowing for a nice campsite. Snow covered the ground here, but they could brush it aside easily enough.

The guide motioned to the spot. "This'll be a good place to wait out the storm, even if it takes a few days."

Relief eased the ache in Eric's bones. As much as he wanted to reach Washington before his father passed, if he died on the journey, that would do neither of his parents any good.

Nor Naomi and Mary Ellen.

Had she received his letter yet? Did she understand the depth of his love? The surety that he *would* be coming back to her? As long as he didn't perish in this snowstorm, that was.

Eric dismounted with a groan, his legs stiff from the ride and the cold that had numbed him all the way down to his feet.

Silas was already directing Harvey on where to clear snow for the fire and their blankets. He motioned toward the horses as he spoke to Eric. "Help me get them unloaded, then the two of you can tie them out while I start us a fire. Make sure you pack ice around the mare's ankle."

The poor horse that had been Harvey's mount had seemed better after the night of rest while they waited out the snow-storm on the open plain. Silas had suggested they swap her with the pack horse, so she didn't have to carry Harvey's greater weight. Harvey hadn't been pleased with that change, but he went along with it when Silas mentioned his other choice was to walk the horse, trudging through knee-deep snow.

Even with the lesser burden, the injured mare's limp had continued all day yesterday and today. Maybe with a longer rest now while they waited out the storm, she could recover fully.

By the time he and Harvey had the animals fed and tied

where they would be protected from the wind, Silas had a healthy blaze crackling in the center of the cleared area. It continually amazed Eric how the man could build a fire when everything around was wet.

He brushed the wood dust from his hands and groaned as he pushed to his feet. "We'll need a good bit o' wood. Best we all start gatherin'."

The work never seemed to end, but maybe once this part was done, he could settle in beside the fire and thaw his frozen, weary limbs. He had to remember why he was doing this. His father and mother needed him. And as soon as he saw to the details there, he could finally get back to Naomi and Mary Ellen. And they could finally move forward together into the life they all craved.

* * *

*T*he relentless wind stung Naomi's face and blurred her vision with swirling snowflakes, as she rode beside Heidi, with Two Stones ahead and Jonah behind them. It felt like she might never be warm. But at least the horses had been able to manage in the knee-deep snow.

They'd made it three days since passing Fort Benton. Jonah had stored his wagon and team at the livery, renting a horse so they could move faster. How fast were Eric and his group moving? As harsh as a mountain snowstorm could be, the gusts across this open plain never seemed to stop. There was no protection. No break from the unending misery.

They had to push on. It might still take days to catch up with Eric, but surely they would reach trees or hills that would offer a little protection. *Lord, slow them down. Give them a safe place to shelter until we get there.*

They'd all been praying this. Only God's intervention could

make this mission successful. He'd sent her after Eric—she knew that with every part of her. The dreams had been so frequent. So clear. And reality had matched so completely.

If God sent them after Eric, He would help them reach the group. She had to cling to that, no matter how miserable every moment was.

"I think those are trees ahead." Jonah had to shout to be heard above the wind.

Naomi squinted, her eyes watering from the biting cold. She made out a line of darkness emerging through the veil of white. Relief weakened her muscles, but she couldn't let herself relax. If they could just make it to the trees, there would be shelter from this unceasing wind.

She glanced skyward. The low gray clouds made it impossible to tell what time it was. Maybe a little after noon? Far too early to stop, but at least in the forest, the ride would be easier.

The trees became more distinct, and the horses picked up speed on their own. Smart animals.

The moment they stepped under the shelter of branches, the wind faded, it's howl muted. She drew in a deep breath, then eased out her tension with spent air.

"Look." Heidi's voice on her left pulled her gaze that way.

A fire.

Her body tensed as she worked to make out the scene. A campfire blazed through the trees ahead. A tent or some sort of cover had been erected nearby. And figures.

Two Stones threw up a hand to halt them.

She jerked back on her reins, a delayed reaction she should have thought of when she first saw the fire.

Was this Eric? Or some other stranger taking refuge from the weather? They would likely be friendly, but until that fact was certain, best not to charge in on them.

Two Stones and Jonah rode forward slowly while she and

Heidi waited. She couldn't make out who the figures were, though there looked to be two or three of them.

Lord, let us have caught up to Eric.

Her insides churned at the thought she would face Harvey again. But Eric would be there. She had to face the truth. Had to let the truth be known, if she and Eric were to ever reach the life together they craved.

Jonah's voice called ahead. "Hello? Eric, is that you?"

Her middle clenched. This really might be it. *God, help me.* She couldn't find other words, but these captured her need fully. She couldn't get through this without Divine strength carrying her.

"Jonah? Two Stones?" Eric's voice sent a flood of relief through her chest. "What are you doing here?"

She nudged her horse forward. She had to get to him. To see with her eyes that he was well. Unhurt from the storm and all the dangers it brought.

Heidi followed behind her and the men's voices sounded ahead, but she couldn't decipher their words with the swish of her horse's hooves in the snow and the squeak of her saddle. Not to mention the distant howl of the wind and her heart pounding in her ears.

But now she could make out the figures ahead. Three men stood around the campfire. An older fellow who must be their guide. The instant her gaze caught on Harvey, she jerked it away.

And there, in the center of it all...Eric.

Emotion surged to her eyes, and she kicked her horse to go faster. At the edge of the camp, she leaped from her saddle.

Eric swung her into his arms, nearly crushing her with the strength of his embrace.

She hugged him back, breathing in his scent—woodsmoke and that unique scent that was his alone. The warmth of him.

Solid, well, and really here. The strength in his arms that always made her feel so safe and protected.

That thought raised a niggle that pulled her back to reality.

His cousin. She had to tell Eric—tell them all—what he'd done.

She pulled back from Eric's hold and made the mistake of glancing at his face. Such concern in those beautiful eyes.

"What's wrong? Didn't you get my letter?" His gaze slid to Jonah, then returned to hers.

Her body began to tremble, but she couldn't weaken now. She had to stay strong for this confession. She took in a breath and glanced at Harvey. Her body reacted to the sight of him with a jerk she couldn't control. He didn't belong out here in this wilderness where she'd found sanctuary.

Yet his narrow-eyed glare gave her the push she needed.

She stepped back from Eric, though not so far that he couldn't keep one hand at her back. She raised her voice enough for all to hear, but spoke to Eric. "I came because I had to warn you. You can't trust what Harvey says. If he came all the way out here, it's because he wants something from you. He's not here to help you, I can promise you that. He'll take whatever he can get, no matter who he hurts." Her voice broke on those last words.

Eric stepped close again, wrapping his arm around her. "Didn't you get my letter? My father's ill. Dying maybe. That's why I'm going east. I'll be back, though. Harvey just came to tell me."

Anger sluiced through her in such a rush that her veins felt like they might explode. Though her whole body trembled, she wouldn't back down.

She faced Harvey, whose eyes were hard as flint and filled with hatred. His hands were clenched like he was itching to strangle her.

She had to speak before he tried to silence her.

She turned to Eric and locked his gaze. "Three weeks after you left last year, I received a note saying you'd sent news. That I should come to your family's home. Harvey was the only one there. He brought me inside and..." A weight pressed so hard on her chest, she could barely breathe. "He...forced... He took..." What she tried not to give him. He took everything. Then pushed her out the front door, sending her crying, broken, terrified.

Eric's voice came low and hard. "Naomi. Are you saying what I think you're saying? Did he...?"

She wouldn't look away from Eric's gaze, no matter how the shame pressed in. He had to see. Had to understand.

As he searched her eyes, she could see the progression of his emotions. Confirmation. Horror. Anger. A rage so intense, his eyes turned solid black.

His hand around her had already tightened, but now it felt like a steal band. He turned to Harvey, and when he spoke, his voice sounded like someone else's. Deep. Impenetrable. Sharp. Likely a finely honed ax.

"Is this true?" There was no question in how Eric spoke the words. Only accusation. Perhaps a single chance for Harvey to speak his side.

Harvey seemed to vacillate between his options—deny the charge and try to wheedle back to his cousin's good graces, or unleash his venom.

Eric must have caught the conflicting expression, for he ground out, "The truth."

The air in the campsite turned stifling, as she caught movement at both sides of her gaze. Jonah on one side and Two Stones and the guide on the other—all of them edging in toward Harvey as if they planned to tackle him.

Harvey's gaze narrowed, and his expression turned to such cold loathing, she wanted to curl behind Eric. She wouldn't cower or run this time, though. She stood her ground.

"The twit should have known better than to be alone with a man. Her reputation was already ruined, I figured I might as well get some pleasure out of her." His brows rose in a snakelike smile. "Besides, it wasn't anything you hadn't already done, oh, perfect cousin."

CHAPTER 24

*F*ury surged through Eric. He wanted to charge forward and punish him for what he'd done to Naomi, and he wanted to whisk Naomi as far from his degenerate cousin as he could get. Naomi, who trembled like a leaf in a windstorm. If he left her side, would she crumble?

In that moment of indecision, Harvey reached into his pocket and pulled out a pistol, aiming it directly at Eric.

Eric's breath froze, and he shifted, moving in front of Naomi as much as he could without drawing attention to her.

Jonah had started toward Harvey, but he jerked to a halt, his arms moving away from his sides.

Eric couldn't see Two Stones and Heidi behind him, but they were there. In danger now, because he'd been a fool.

A thick dread hung in the air.

"Move over. Away from him. Or else I'll shoot him first and you next." Harvey's voice bit out the words as he glared at Naomi. Surely she wouldn't do it. Harvey had to be bluffing about shooting them both. Or at least she would think so. That crazed look in his cousin's eyes was so foreign from anything Eric had ever seen there.

Movement at the corner of his gaze made him shift to look. Naomi. She'd stepped completely away from his body.

She spoke, her voice hard with fury. "There's no need to hurt us both."

No, no, no, no, no! Why was she trying to protect him?

He had to stop Harvey. *Lord, don't let him shoot. Please. Don't let him hurt her again.*

It was Jonah who spoke next, his voice low and calming. "You'd better think twice before you fire that thing. Seems to me, taking a life would only make the situation worse for you."

Harvey sneered, though he didn't shift his gaze—or his aim—from Naomi.

Naomi lifted her chin a little, revealing the courage she carried with such grace.

Lord, give her strength. No matter what, don't let that bullet hit her. Protect her.

How had it come to this? Harvey, the cousin he'd played with like a brother through their entire childhood. The man he was now training to take a leading role in their family's company. Harvey had done the worst of crimes to Naomi—the reminder sent fresh fury through his veins—and now he was threatening to kill her?

What had Naomi done to anger him so?

Naomi had been right. Harvey must have been the one who'd blocked their letters and telegrams from reaching each other. Like a heel, Eric had waved her concern aside. Fresh pain sliced through him. She'd had every reason to suspect Harvey. The man had already shown her the depths of his depravity.

And Eric hadn't believed her. *Dear God, forgive me.*

Now, all he could do was make it right. Face down his cousin and stop this evil. "Why are you doing this, Harvey? Is it me you're angry with?"

His cousin still didn't shift his gaze from Naomi, but a fresh hatred dirtied his eyes. "You've always thought you were better than me. You and your rich family. You take whatever you want without a care for what you do to those around you. Even those you call friends. When they can't give what you want anymore, you toss 'em out like scraps for the pigs."

Bile churned in his gut. Was Harvey speaking truth? If he had real examples... "When have I done that?"

Harvey's voice lost all inflection. "Nathan."

Eric's heart froze, then pumped pain through him. "Nathan?" His voice came out too weak. Too uncertain. He was supposed to be fighting for Naomi. Protecting her. But Nathan... His biggest regret, other than the indiscretion with Heidi, was that day he'd led Nathan and Harvey up the rocky mountainside where they'd been warned not to go.

"You took his life from him. He was smarter than you. Stronger than you. Better than you. And you didn't like it. You took his future and left him a shell of himself. Confined to a chair for the rest of his life. So addled he can't even read or write."

Eric forced the truth through the desert his throat had become. "I didn't do that to Nathan. The rockslide did. He was my best friend. I would have given my life to stop him from getting hurt."

"Is that why you ran like a scared little boy, only worried about yourself?"

Eric wanted to drop to his knees, cover his head and weep. He *had* been a scared boy. Panicked. Yet that didn't change the monumental results of his disobedience that day.

Life-changing, as Harvey said.

"Because of you, my—" A flash from the side cut off Harvey's words.

Jonah charged him, and Harvey swiveled to protect himself.

The gun exploded, a puff of powder clouding the tip.

Eric launched at Harvey and tackled him.

Two Stones grabbed his gun hand and jerked it away.

Though Harvey struggled, the two of them subdued him, flipping him onto his belly in the snow. From the corner of Eric's eye, he could see Silas standing before them rifle in hand, pointed toward Harvey. Relief allowed him a moment to breathe. "We need rope."

Silas nodded. "I'll get it."

As the man stepped backward, weapon still aimed at their captive, Eric saw what was behind him.

The women were crouched over a form laid out in the snow. *Jonah.*

* * *

*B*lood everywhere.

Naomi's pulse raced as she knelt with Heidi at Jonah's side. What should she do?

Jonah gripped his shoulder, rolling onto his side as he groaned with pain. "I'm...all right."

But he clearly wasn't.

The bullet had struck his right shoulder. Was there a main artery through there? She couldn't remember. But maybe the one that went up through the neck.

She had to stop the bleeding.

Jonah was curled onto the injured side, so she couldn't get at it.

She gripped his good shoulder. "Lay back."

Jonah started to move, but not to lie flat. He pushed like he was trying to sit upright. "I'm..." A deep grunt broke through his words as he reached a sitting position.

He whooshed out a breath, then heaved another in, taking in loud, lung-filling breaths as he recovered from the effort. He still gripped his shoulder, and she could see it better now.

Blood saturated Jonah's coat over the entire shoulder and had turned his hand crimson. Naomi glanced at Heidi, hoping she'd step in and take charge. Her face had lost its color, and she didn't back away. Nor did she offer instructions.

Naomi was the one who'd been raised by her doctor grandfather, whose twin sister was a talented physician. She should know what to do.

She reached for the flap of Jonah's coat. "We're going to slide your arm out of this so we can stop the bleeding." He would be cold, but if he lost too much blood, keeping him warm wouldn't save his life.

Jonah shifted to give her access, his face twisted in pain.

She unfastened the buttons. She'd never undressed a man, not even to take off his outer coat. She glanced up to where Eric and Two Stones held Harvey in the snow. The guide was with them now, crouching as they talked. They had things in hand there, and as far as she knew, none of the men had much doctoring experience. *Help me, God.*

Her frozen, clumsy fingers took too long, but at last she had the coat unfastened. When she peeled the garment off his shoulder, Jonah's face scrunched even more. She hated to be the cause of so much pain.

Blood plastered his shirt to the muscle beneath, and the bullet hole gaped like a dark eye. She'd half expected to see blood bubbling out of the wound, but that wasn't the case. Was it still bleeding? His shirt was so soaked, it was hard to tell.

She should press fabric against the spot to stop the flow, if there was one. She grabbed Jonah's coat and pressed the inside lining to his shoulder.

"Let's see what's happening over here." The guide's voice beside her nearly made her jump.

He crouched down and peered at Jonah's shoulder. He must be at least fifty, maybe more. He was so grizzled from years in the elements, it was hard to tell. Maybe he knew a bit about doctoring. He certainly didn't seem ruffled by Jonah's injury.

"He was shot in the shoulder. I'm trying to stop the blood."

He probably already knew those things, but she couldn't think of anything else to say. Nothing helpful anyway.

"Yer doin' it well. Would ye mind if'n I take a look? I've nursed a few gunshot wounds through the years." Though his voice was as weathered as his face, his respectful way of offering help eased a little of her tension.

"Here." She eased backward, keeping the coat pressed to his shoulder until the man could take over. "I'm Naomi Wyatt, by the way. And this is Jonah Coulter. And Heidi." She fumbled with each introduction. Civilities were the least of their worries just now, but it would help if they all knew each other's names.

The guide took over applying pressure to the wound, then eased in as Naomi vacated the spot. "Pleasure to meet ya. Name's Silas Grant."

He peeled the coat away slowly, peering underneath. At last, he revealed the bloody shirt and dark hole. He shifted to look at Jonah's back, then moved around to study the wound. "Jonah, son. Reckon the bullet's pressin' a nerve or two in there. That's why it's extra painful. Hang on a moment an' we'll see what we can do for it." He reached to his side and lifted a long hunting knife.

Naomi sucked in a breath, and Jonah jerked backward. "You're not poking that thing in me."

Mr. Grant chuckled. "Naw. Just need to cut yer shirt open a bit. I won't get the skin, you can count on it."

Jonah moved back to his position, though he eyed the blade with a narrow-eyed glare.

Naomi hovered nearby as Mr. Grant examined the wound. A few steps away, Eric and Two Stones finally stood. Harvey lay on his belly in the snow, hands and ankles bound, with a rope connecting them together.

Eric turned and met her gaze, but then his focus scanned the rest of their scene, and a frown twisted his expression. "He was shot?"

Naomi pushed to her feet and stepped away from Jonah so she could share the details with Eric and Two Stones. Before she spoke a word, Eric reached her and wrapped his arms around her.

She'd not planned to fall into his arms, but the moment he offered his support, she clung to him. Her body laid down its defenses, allowing the fear and vulnerability and pain to pour out of her. Tears burned her eyes and warmed her cheeks.

Eric wrapped his hands around her, one at her back, the other cradling her head. "I'm sorry. I'm so, so sorry." His murmur wove through her, adding strength where she was weakest. She couldn't fully vent her emotions now, not with Jonah injured and all these people around. But at least she could let herself fully comprehend that she was safe.

Harvey couldn't hurt her again. God had stopped him, using Jonah and all these wonderful people.

She squeezed her eyes shut. *Thank you.* Then she inhaled a long, steadying breath, and when she exhaled, she let the turmoil of emotions flow out with the spent air.

She eased back from Eric. He seemed reluctant to let her go, but she didn't plan to go far, just far enough to turn to see what was happening with Jonah. When she did, Eric kept one arm around her waist.

She sniffed and cleared her throat. "Mr. Grant said he's nursed gunshot wounds before."

The man sat back on his heels and sent a glance her way. "Call me Silas, ma'am. I can get the bullet out, and it'll bring some relief. It's gonna hurt like hell fire while I'm doin' it, though. The other option's to head back to Fort Benton an' find the doctor there."

Pain had etched deep lines at the corners of Jonah's eyes and shadows beneath them. "What would you do if you were me?"

"I'll do my best to make sure I get everything out. There's a chance the wound'll fester, but there's more of a chance of that if'n we leave the bullet in. And that's prob'ly what's painin' the most. The hardest part is the hurt while I'm workin'."

The weight on Naomi's chest made it hard to breathe. This was Jonah's choice, but letting a mountain man dig a bullet out of his shoulder? New tears pressed at just the thought of how horrible that would feel. Would he use his hunting knife? Dinah was always so meticulous about keeping her doctoring tools clean.

"Mr., ah...Silas?" When he turned to her, she pressed on. "Have you dug a bullet from flesh before? How would you do it?"

He dipped his chin in a nod. "Yes'm. Probably half a dozen times, though only once in the shoulder. I've a kit I picked up in Benton from a gunsmith. Use it to keep my Hawkins in good order, but it's got the right little tools I need fer this kinda work."

At least he wouldn't be digging with the tip of his bloodied knife. He did seem to have experience. She turned to Jonah, who was watching her with pai- clouded eyes. That pain would be much worse while Silas worked, but then maybe he could start healing. She did her best fill her gaze with encouragement. "Seems that'd be the best decision."

He turned back to Silas. "Get it done."

CHAPTER 25

*E*ric stood at the edge of camp, watching the group settle in for the night. They'd built a second campfire so everyone could stay warm, and it heated his frontside. He should move closer. He should join them.

But too much unrest still coiled in his body to bed down.

Jonah's surgery had been awful.

Silas had sent the women to tend the horses while Eric and Two Stones held Jonah down. Coulter took the pain like a man, no doubt about it, keeping his jaw locked tight, though his face turned white and sweat trickled down his skin. There near the end, Silas must have pressed on a nerve, for Jonah bellowed, then passed out from the pain.

Small mercy, that.

Poor fellow. He came to as Silas was wrapping the shoulder with the extra shirt they'd found in Jonah's saddle pack. Now, he lay bundled in his bedroll between the fires, sleeping once more.

At least the worst was behind him. *Let that be so, Lord.*

No matter how strong Eric wanted to be, seeing all this pain ate at him. He stared into the fire as Naomi's confession replayed. Once they had Harvey tied to a tree with a rifle aimed at him, he'd admitted to interfering with the letters and telegrams. He'd even come all this way and lied about Eric's father's illness, just to get Eric to come back with him. His plan had been shrewd, even paying off a clerk in the telegraph office back home to respond to Eric's wire with more of the same falsehood. Of course, he'd not accounted for the river freezing and the treacherous conditions involved in a journey overland.

Could it really all have been about jealousy? Separating him and Naomi, inflicting such pain on her, then coming all this way to the Montana Territory just to tear them apart again? Only a madman could develop such a hatred he'd be willing to tear apart lives, including his own.

Naomi had been the one to suffer the most. Even now, he wanted to stride over to where his cousin sat tied to a tree and pummel him into unconsciousness.

That wouldn't help Naomi though. *Help me, God. Help me be the man she needs me to be. And show me what that is.*

As though he'd called her with his thoughts, Naomi stood from where she'd been rummaging through her pack and came toward him. Weariness lined her eyes, pressing another weight over his spirit. She looked like she might appreciate comfort. He would give all he had to offer.

When he opened his arms, she stepped into them, leaning on him as though her legs couldn't bear the weight any longer. He soaked in the warmth of her, the softness, the rich scent of her hair. The feeling of home that always eased through him with Naomi in his arms.

He let his cheek rest on her head, breathing deeply to fully experience this moment. He would do anything for thousands more like it. Naomi and Mary Ellen were the best part of him. He'd thought he knew that before, but after the threat of losing Naomi, of knowing how deeply his own cousin had hurt her, he could see things so much more clearly. If Naomi wanted to stay in the mountains, he'd make his life there too. His father would have to understand. Wasn't there a verse in Scripture that talked about how a man should leave his father and mother and be united with his wife?

More than anything, Eric wanted to be united with this woman, their lives woven together with God as their center. A three-strand cord that could never be broken.

In his arms, Naomi inhaled deeply, which was followed by a shuddering exhale. Was she crying, or simply letting out pent-up tension?

He stroked her back with his fingertips. He needed to bring up what Harvey did and apologize for his own blindness. They hadn't had a chance to talk since she told him, and the last thing he wanted was for this to become an invisible boulder between them, something they never spoke of.

"Naomi." He kept his voice just loud enough that only she could hear him. "I'm sorry. So sorry for what my cousin did. For all you've had to endure." His voice broke, but he pressed on. "I'm sorry I wasn't there when you needed me. I'm sorry we've missed out on our life together. And I'm sorry I didn't believe you when you told me Harvey was the one intercepting our letters."

Did he feel her tremble? He tucked her a little closer, pressing his warmth around her. Wrapping her in his love. "You're my love. My heart. And it tears me up that I wasn't there to protect you."

Her shoulders lifted as she took in another deep breath, and he eased his hold a little so she had room to breathe. But she burrowed deeper in his arms. Maybe air wasn't as important as comfort right now.

Heal her wounds, Lord. Give her the comfort of the Spirit that Jesus promised. He kept up a steady litany of prayers as he held her.

When finally Naomi spoke, her voice was a whisper barely

audible above the crackling of the fire and the distant sounds of the night settling around them. "I've forgiven Harvey." She sniffed, giving him a moment to take in his words.

How could she possibly forgive the vile things his cousin did to her? Naomi was strong, but this seemed impossible even for her.

She spoke again, her tone a little more solid. "Not because he deserves it, but because I can't let the bitterness build. If I did, I would never be what Mary Ellen needs me to be."

So much emotion welled in Eric's throat that he couldn't speak. This woman never ceased to inspire him. Mary Ellen was blessed to have such a mother. He was even more blessed to be holding her here, this night. Certainty spread through him. They'd wasted too much time already.

Eric loosened his grip just enough to tilt Naomi's face toward his, needing to see her beautiful brown eyes. A sliver of moonlight painted a silver glow on her features, revealing a shimmer still in her gaze.

"You are..." He struggled for words that would do justice to what she inspired in him. "You are grace embodied, Naomi. Your strength humbles me."

Her expression softened, giving him courage to continue. "God has brought us through so much, and I don't want another day to go by where we're not building our life together. If you'll let me, I want to spend my life protecting and loving you and Mary Ellen, working to be the man you need me to be. We can stay in the mountains, if that's where you want to be. Near your sister and all these people who are like family." Like family to her, and hopefully soon to him.

Naomi didn't answer, and her hesitation worried him. She'd said she would marry him. But that was before this awful event with Harvey. Had she changed her mind? Or perhaps she needed more time to heal. He would give her whatever she needed. Maybe he should say that.

Before he could, though, a watery smile eased over her features. "I want to be with you, Eric. I've come to love these mountains, but I love you more. Now that God brought us back together, I want my home to be with you and Mary Ellen, wherever that is."

He breathed in the joy. The relief. The peace and rightness of it all.

This woman. *You've given me so much more than I ever thought possible, God.*

He returned his own grin. "We can pray about where God wants us."

His gaze dipped to her mouth, but he forced it back to her eyes. She might not want a kiss so soon after reliving what Harvey had done. He couldn't let his own desires rush her.

But her eyes had darkened with a hunger he knew well.

He lowered his mouth—slowly, gently—and brushed her lips with his. A kiss to seal his promise.

Lord willing, the first of so many to come.

EPILOGUE

*E*ric stood in the bunkhouse, staring down at the telegram, taking in the message so unexpected. Such a unique and wonderful answer to his prayers.

He'd unfolded this paper to read the words so many times on the journey back from Fort Benton to the Coulter Ranch that the paper was crinkled and smudged from being gripped by snow-dampened fingers.

Now, as he prepared for the wedding ceremony with Naomi, the depth of God's blessing nearly made him weak. Everything he and Naomi had been through had led them to this point.

Once they'd all made it back to Fort Benton, Two Stones and Silas helped him take Harvey to the law office. The deputy there said they'd hold him in a cell until the circuit judge came through for a proper trial.

That had been hard, leaving his cousin, the man Eric had thought was one of his closest friends—close as a brother—through the years. Yet Harvey had to face the consequences of what he'd done. Eric had a soon-to-be bride and daughter to protect.

They'd stayed a few days in town, both so Jonah could rest

and be tended by the doctor there, and also because he needed to exchange telegrams with his father. He'd used a different telegraph office this time, farther from his parents' home, but where no bribed clerk could send a false reply.

His first message had been to make sure his father wasn't actually ill. Dad had confirmed his health with his usual statement—*In my prime.* If the cost for each word in a telegram weren't so steep, he surely would have finished with, *even at the youthful age of two-and-fifty.*

Then Eric told his father about Naomi and Mary Ellen, that he and Naomi were to be married. He'd promised to send a letter with news about Harvey, but most importantly, he said he wouldn't be returning to Washington and that he needed to step back from the business completely. That had been a hard message to send, and Naomi had done her best to distract him for the hours it took to receive a reply.

The return message had been written on the paper he held in his hand.

Timing couldn't be better. Thinking of selling company, splitting profit. Retirement for me, income for you until next endeavor.

The relief still raised a well of emotion in Eric's chest. Not only had God created the perfect route for him to pull back from the business and his parents to have income for the rest of their years, but this would also allow Eric to purchase what he needed to start this new life in these Montana mountains with Naomi and Mary Ellen.

Jericho had welcomed his request to build a cabin in the clearing where they'd had the picnic. The men all offered their help in building it. Even Jonah, though he'd have to do lighter work until his shoulder healed. They were welcoming him in, something he'd not thought possible that first day on the ranch.

"Eric?" Jonah's voice sounded from the bunkhouse doorway, tugging him from his thoughts.

Eric slipped the telegram back into the Bible on his bed, then turned to the man. "Is it time?"

Jonah stepped in and closed the door, an act that sent a ripple of unease through Eric. Did he still harbor a bit of anger at losing Naomi? Surely, he wouldn't attempt to start an altercation now. Jonah had become a good friend these past weeks.

But perhaps he wanted one final chance to say his piece. He deserved that.

Jonah stood a few steps away, scrubbing a hand over the back of his neck. "I, uh, just wanted to say…I've been praying that God blesses your marriage. With Naomi." He finally lifted his gaze to Eric's, and earnestness shone in his eyes. A bit of hurt, too, perhaps, but Jonah possessed strength and integrity, no doubt about it.

"Thank you." Those words seemed far too paltry for the depth of his appreciation. "You're a good man, and your friendship means a lot."

Jonah nodded. He didn't seem to know what to say next, his boots scuffing the floor.

Eric cleared his throat. "So…what's next for you?" The moment the words slipped out, he wanted to call them back. Jonah didn't have to have a *next*. He worked the ranch with his brothers. That was his life.

But Jonah didn't seem bothered. "Thought I'd head out in a few days if the weather holds. Follow up on those leads from the passenger lists. Maybe I can find Anna's aunt."

Eric nodded, though he hated the thought of Naomi facing another separation, this time from the child they had both come to love as their own. But he forced himself to say, "That's a good idea."

Jonah straightened and turned toward the door. "Well, I reckon' it's probably time to head up there."

Eric followed him out, anticipation building as they started up the hill to where the group had gathered in the open area beside the house. Naomi said this was where Dinah and Jericho had been married, with a view of the mountain peaks rising in the distance.

The afternoon sun shone surprisingly warm from a sky as clear and blue as he'd ever seen. The entire Coulter clan had gathered, as well as Two Stones, Heidi, and Two Stones's parents. The ride from their village must be harder for them, with their advanced age, yet they'd come for this special day.

When Eric and Jonah reached the group, Eric aimed toward the minister who had come all the way from Missoula for the occasion. The man's kind eyes and leathery smile seemed perfect for a ceremony in this beautiful yet challenging country.

"Thank you for coming." Eric clasped the man's hand. Before he could respond, a hush fell over the people gathered behind him.

Eric turned, his heart picking up speed as he searched for his intended.

A figure emerged from the house, and his heart knew it was Naomi before his eyes could be certain in the bright sunlight. She stepped from the stoop and turned toward him, revealing her radiant smile. She held Mary Ellen in the crook of her arm, the child's red curls reflecting the sunlight as if aflame. On Naomi's other side, she'd linked arms with her sister. She'd said Dinah planned to walk with her in place of their father. He could only hope Naomi wasn't missing her parents and grandparents too much on this day.

For his part, so much awe filled his chest as he watched his bride and their daughter approach, he couldn't imagine anything could make this day more perfect.

As Naomi approached, her gaze never strayed from his. He couldn't have looked away if he wanted to. She was so...beautiful...it hurt. Yet he'd welcome this intense ache for the rest of his life.

Dinah placed a hand on his arm, forcing his attention away from Naomi. She gave him a pointed smile. "Eric, I give my sister and niece into your care with trust and love. May the Lord bless your family abundantly."

He swallowed, letting his gaze flick to Naomi and Mary Ellen before returning to meet Dinah's gaze. "I will protect and cherish them all my days."

Dinah nodded, and her smile turned tender as she pressed a kiss to her sister's cheek. He didn't catch the words she whispered, but they brought a glimmer of emotion to Naomi's eyes.

Dinah joined Eric and Naomi's hands, then stepped away.

Eric linked his fingers with his bride's, then rubbed the back of her hand with his thumb. The smile she blessed him with warmed his insides. He lifted her hand so he could press a kiss to the place his thumb had just rubbed. This woman had fought her way into his heart with unwavering courage and a love that humbled him.

The minister cleared his throat gently, signaling the beginning of the ceremony. Naomi passed Mary Ellen into Dinah's waiting arms, and the two of them turned to make the vows that would begin their life together.

A family at last.

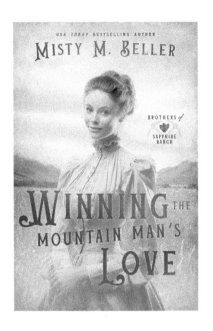

Get WINNING THE MOUNTAIN MAN'S LOVE, the next book in the Brothers of Sapphire Ranch series, at your favorite retailer!

Did you enjoy Eric and Naomi's story? I hope so!
Would you take a quick minute to leave a review where you purchased the book?
It doesn't have to be long. Just a sentence or two telling what you liked about the story!

* * *

To receive a free book and get updates when new Misty M. Beller books release, go to https://mistymbeller.com/freebook

ALSO BY MISTY M. BELLER

Call of the Rockies

Freedom in the Mountain Wind

Hope in the Mountain River

Light in the Mountain Sky

Courage in the Mountain Wilderness

Faith in the Mountain Valley

Honor in the Mountain Refuge

Peace in the Mountain Haven

Grace on the Mountain Trail

Calm in the Mountain Storm

Joy on the Mountain Peak

Brides of Laurent

A Warrior's Heart

A Healer's Promise

A Daughter's Courage

Hearts of Montana

Hope's Highest Mountain

Love's Mountain Quest

Faith's Mountain Home

Honor's Mountain Promise

Texas Rancher Trilogy

The Rancher Takes a Cook

The Ranger Takes a Bride

The Rancher Takes a Cowgirl

Wyoming Mountain Tales

A Pony Express Romance

ABOUT THE AUTHOR

Misty M. Beller is a *USA Today* best-selling author of romantic mountain stories, set on the 1800s frontier and woven with the truth of God's love.

Raised on a farm and surrounded by family, Misty developed her love for horses, history, and adventure. These days, her husband and children provide fresh adventure every day, keeping her both grounded and crazy.

Misty's passion is to create inspiring Christian fiction infused with the grandeur of the mountains, writing historical romance that displays God's abundant love through the twists and turns in the lives of her characters.

Sharing her stories with readers is a dream come true for Misty. She writes from her country home in South Carolina and escapes to the mountains any chance she gets.

Connect with Misty at <u>www.MistyMBeller.com</u>

Milton Keynes UK
Ingram Content Group UK Ltd.
UKHW012337010424
440454UK00002B/12